LUCILLE TRAVIS

THE FAR JOURNEY

journeyforth®

Greenville, South Carolina

Library of Congress Cataloging-in-Publication Data

Travis, Lucille, date.
   The Far Journey / Lucille Travis.
          p. cm.
   Summary: Horace, who recently reached mousehood, is caught
breaking an important rule and awaiting punishment when a dire
situation proves him a hero, but he feels compelled to leave the
idyllic Fleur Gardens community to seek his long-lost mother and
brother, accompanied by good friends.
   ISBN 978-1-60682-023-0 (perfect bound pbk. : alk. paper)
   [1. Heroes—Fiction. 2. Conduct of life—Fiction. 3. Mice—Fiction. 4.
Community life—Fiction. 5. Voyages and travels—Fiction.]   I. Title.
   PZ7.T68915Far 2009
   [Fic]—dc22
                                                   2009017094

The Far Journey
Illustrations by Guy Porfirio
Design and page layout by Nick Ng

© 2009 by BJU Press
Greenville, SC 29614
JourneyForth Books is a division of BJU Press

15   14   13   12   11   10   9   8   7   6   5   4   3   2   1

To Georgia,
our second granddaughter, whose merry heart and
loving ways delight all your family. You have always loved
stories, and so this story is for you.

May it remind you that every day is waiting for your
footsteps, and may you see the path Jesus has made just
for you. I love you, Georgia, and thank you for the sweet
songs you sing with your sister, songs that stay in my heart.

CONTENTS

CHAPTER 1

In the darkness, snow fell steadily covering the private grounds and piling on top of the iron gate closed across the entrance. A large brick building stood alone in the center of the park-like grounds. The road leading to it was already lost beneath the snow, the lampposts along its sides sticking up out of the drifts their lamps barely visible. All but one of the building's twelve floors of labs and offices were dark. On the first floor, night-lights cast a dim glow through the glass wall of the Fleur Gardens Restaurant. The faint light was enough for two well-armed rats who peered from behind the snow-covered branches of a nearby bush. As they watched the mice of Fleur Gardens feasting inside the restaurant's grand dining room, the older rat made a low hissing sound through clenched teeth. His companion's eyes narrowed, "Aye, Captain, they'll be singing a different tune soon enough."

Unaware of the watchers, Horace brushed a crumb of cherry cake from his gray fur, leaned back against a red velvet chair cushion, and sighed contentedly. From now on he would no longer be thought of as a youngster.

"Here's to mousehood," he said holding up his acorn cup of cherry-mint tea. Horace looked lazily at his best friend Max, who nodded and drank deeply from his own hand-carved acorn cup.

Across from the two younger mice, Mr. Baxter twitched his whiskers with pleasure. "Ahem," he said. "Now that you have reached mousehood, you will surely want to think about your futures, and I wish you the very best." Mr. Baxter smiled and was silent for a moment. "But first, Horace, my boy, there is something I need to tell you." With a solemn look on his white whiskered face he placed a small package in Horace's paw. "Please open it carefully, lad," he urged.

Slowly Horace removed the paper wrapping from the unexpected gift. At last it lay in his paw, a thin white ivory carving. Puzzled, he examined it closely. It was jagged on one side and straight on the other. He turned it over. "Strange," he said. "I'm afraid I can't guess. What is it?"

Mr. Baxter took the carving in his own paw and held it up. "See here," he said pointing, "how one side forms the outline of a tree while the other side is straight and rough? I believe it is a maple tree, but only one half of the tree."

"So it seems," Max remarked.

"I see it now," Horace said. "But what happened to it?"

Mr. Baxter held the carving up. "This once belonged to your mother. On the day she brought you here to Fleur Gardens and left you in our care, she also left this. You were but a mouseling then, too young to know what was happening. When she left, she entrusted this to me. If she did not return for you, it was to be given to you on your mousehood birthday."

"Today," Horace whispered.

Mr. Baxter placed the carving back in Horace's paw. "Your brother has the other half," he said.

Horace stared at him. "My brother? You're saying I have a brother? Where is he?" he demanded. "Why wasn't I told I had a brother?" He glared at Mr. Baxter accusingly. The ivory clutched in his paw dug into him, but he ignored the pain.

"We do not know where your brother may be. Sadly, your brother was lost after the great fire in your city. When your mother carried you both to safety in a nearby abandoned box car, she placed one half of the necklace on your brother and the other half on you just in case you were separated later. There were so many families fleeing the ruins—so many injured—that while she was gone to help others, your brother wandered off. She tried to find him, but after looking everywhere for two days, she brought you here where you would be safe while she continued to search." Mr. Baxter paused and cleared his throat.

"Your mother gave me your half of the necklace to hold for you. If she did not return, I was to see that you were told nothing of your brother's disappearance until you were old enough to understand and make wise choices. That is what mousehood is all about, and today you have reached mousehood. And so I have kept this for you until now." Mr. Baxter's eyes grew sad. Gently he touched the carving with his paw.

Horace loosened his hold on the carving. "She never came back for me. If she lived, she surely would have come."

Mr. Baxter rose from his seat. "I fear so," he said. "I can only trust that you will honor her memory and prove to be the wise son she hoped for. Your mother gave you the only gift she could, Horace, when she brought you here to safety. Hers was a noble act."

"But what should I do?" Horace searched Mr. Baxter's kindly old face, his dark eyes, and thinning whiskers. "You've been my teacher, my friend. Tell me. Am I to leave here and search for this brother?" He held up the broken tree. "My mother must have told you what she wanted me to do."

"Do?" Mr. Baxter shook his head, "No, no. It was the very thing she would *not* have said. She wanted you to know these things when you were old enough to understand, old enough to make wise choices. None of us knows all that happened the night of that fire. It was a long time ago, Horace. Sadly, it is likely we may never know." Mr. Baxter touched Horace's shoulder gently. "It's late, almost curfew time. Better finish up. Good night to you both." When he had gone, the room seemed thick with silence. Max blew his nose hard and wiped his whiskers.

Horace looked through the glass wall of the dimly lit restaurant. Drifts of snow continued to pile against the glass as Horace watched. A slight movement caught his eye, but when he looked he saw only the falling snow and darkness beyond. "Max, what if my mother did find my brother, but she couldn't get back here? They might be out there somewhere right now."

"It's been many years, mate," Max said. "Sad as it is, if your brother did survive, he may not even know about you." Max blew his nose again.

"I've always thought I was an orphan, like you, Max," Horace said. In his mind he tried to picture his mother. What if she hadn't died? Why hadn't she come back for him? Snow slapped against the window catching his attention. He couldn't help imagining his mother and his brother lost somewhere in a storm like this one and struggling to make their way to safety. A sudden movement outside startled him. There was someone out there!

"Max," he cried, "look by that tree. Do you see them?" He could barely make out the two snow-covered figures inching their way along.

Max scrambled to his feet. "You don't suppose . . . ?" Max didn't finish his sentence. Horace was already running through the restaurant archway that opened into its indoor gardens. Outside the restaurant, the first floor had been turned into a massive garden of flowers, lush plants, and small trees that sloped gently upwards to border the staircase leading to the second floor. Hidden beneath the gardens were the tunnels, burrows, and meeting rooms of the Fleur Gardens Mice.

At the edge of the garden patio a team of mice were gleaning the day's leftovers from under tables and behind chairs as Horace and Max raced by. Several young mice, glad to be out of the underground tunnels, were tumbling about in patches of wild mint and paid no attention. Their mothers standing nearby frowned at the unexpected interruption.

Horace headed straight to the undergarden tunnel opening that led to the east mouse-gate, the nearest gate to the outside courtyard. It was open. Two of the mice guard stood by it. Horace, breathing hard stopped running. Max caught up with him.

"Sorry," one of the guards said. "Nobody can go out this late. It's nearly curfew time." He stepped in front of Horace and Max. "Besides, there's been a sighting of rats near the building, and the patrol's out looking for them."

"Rats?" Horace said, "But I saw mice out there. Two of them in the courtyard."

"Probably two of the patrol," the guard said. "Nothing we can't handle."

Max pulled at Horace's arm. "Come on, I'll walk you to your place."

Horace backed away. "But I tell you it wasn't the patrol I saw. And I'm sure it was mice not rats," he insisted. The guard rolled his eyes and stood firmly blocking the way. Again Max was pulling Horace's arm, and this time Horace didn't resist. As they walked back, Horace's thoughts raced. He was certain he had seen two figures too small to be rats. "You saw them, Max. You said so. Did they look like patrol to you?"

"We're both jumpy tonight," Max said. "It's late, and I don't know for sure what I saw. It couldn't be mice wandering outside this time of night. The patrols would never allow it."

"Then what? Moles? Too big." Horace pressed a paw against his forehead. Had he imagined he saw two figures because he'd been thinking so hard about his mother and lost brother? "Sorry, Max. Maybe I did imagine more than I saw." He shrugged his shoulders.

Max thumped his back. "Come on, mate, there's still time, and I say we get another mint tea before the stand closes." Behind the restaurant bar a few elderly mice were still drinking spiced cherry tea and talking of the day's news when Horace and Max arrived. Horace ordered two mint teas.

Outside in the dark close to the courtyard, two small figures rested at the base of a pine tree. "You must go on without me, Leta," the old mouse said in a thin, weak voice. Her breath came in rasping sounds. "You will have a better chance alone. Please go," she urged.

The younger mouse tightened her paw on the old one's shoulder. "I will not leave you," she said fiercely. Her dark eyes filled with tears as she looked at her aunt. "If the mice of Fleur Gardens won't take us both, then we'll go on until we find a place. Remember how you always taught me all creatures have their place in this world? We will find ours. Just a little ways more, Aunt Hanna, please." Fighting a wave of exhaustion, she helped her aunt to stand. "Here, lean against my shoulder. There has to be an entrance somewhere," she said. Half-supporting, half-dragging the weight of her aunt, she headed once more into the wind. Aunt Hanna no longer resisted. For many days they had traveled, stopping only to rest in dark alleys or under old bridges, always heading north. Leta frowned as she stared into the night at the great silent building. Even if the stories she'd heard were true, they might not accept her and Aunt Hanna. Some said no such place existed; others said that it did indeed exist, but was well guarded and did not welcome strangers. No matter. They had lost everything in the last rat attack on their community. There was nothing more to lose.

Leta's breath burned her chest. Her body felt numb except for the pain in her shoulder where Aunt Hanna leaned heavily. The sudden cry of "Rats! Over here!" struck deep terror into her heart.

A fierce looking mouse with his weapon raised high rushed towards them. On coming closer he scowled. "Who are you, and where do you think you are going?" he demanded. Leta stared at him unable to speak

Others hurried towards them. A tall broad-shouldered mouse stepped forward. "What's this?" he said. "It seems you're mistaken about our rats, Barga."

The fierce looking mouse lowered his weapon. "Yes sir, Captain."

The captain spoke gently to Leta. "Are you lost? Can we help you?"

Before Leta could answer him. Aunt Hanna whispered, "Fleur Gardens. Is it here? Have we . . . ?" And she fainted away.

The captain caught her as she fell. "Here, you two," he ordered the nearest guards. "Carry her back into the tunnel." He turned to Leta who was ready to fall herself.

"If you will allow me," he said, offering her his arm. "This is indeed Fleur Gardens, and I suggest we make our way inside as quickly as possible, miss."

Curfew sounded, and stifling a yawn Horace waved good night as Max left for his own quarters. Tomorrow he would think what to do about the small, white ivory carving in his pack. He reached his door in the east tunnel just as a patrol came hurrying through the gate at the far end. Two of the guards carried a large bundle wrapped in shawls. Horace stood rigid. He hadn't imagined what he saw. Half-walking, half-carried along by the captain was a young mouse, her fur snow-covered, her head drooping. As they drew closer, Horace leaned against the wall to let them go by. At the gate one of the guards stopped to lock it behind him. Horace recognized Barga and hurried to catch him. "Barga, what's going on? What happened?"

Barga shook his head. "More homeless strangers, and from the looks of the old one she won't last the night. Her daughter doesn't look much better off. Soft-headed the captain is, taking in every stray that comes along. We're already running out of space. Won't hold many more." Barga strode along muttering.

Horace shook his head to clear it, and he settled his glasses firmly on his nose. Whatever he'd been thinking, he was wrong about one of them being his long- lost brother. But who were these two? They'd surely gotten lost, but what had they been doing out in such a storm anyway?

CHAPTER 2

News of the arrival of strangers had spread quickly. The two were recovering from their ordeal, and Horace had not seen them again. He did learn that the young mouse and her elderly aunt were the only survivors of a fierce rat attack on their community. A week had gone by, and tonight there would be a dinner to welcome them. Promptly at seven Horace entered the underground meeting hall where long tables had been set up and found the seat Max had saved for him.

"Thought you might be wanting to sit close to the newcomers, mate," Max said. The seats were near enough to the guest table for Horace to see the face of the elderly stranger. She wore her years well and seemed to have recovered from their journey. Under Horace's neck fur he felt the half of the ivory tree he now wore. If he was ever to find the half that belonged to his brother, he needed to learn all he could about that fire years ago. Maybe the old one knew something about it. Eager to catch every word, he leaned forward as the young mouse named Leta spoke.

She told her story well, though her voice faltered at the end as she said, "After the rats attacked our warehouse, and Aunt Hanna and I came out of hiding, we found nothing left. No one else survived. We set out then to find the mice of Fleur Gardens, hoping yours was a real community and not just the stuff of legends."

Horace sat back, his shoulders slumping. If his brother had been there, he too had not survived.

Leta paused to wipe away a single tear before she went on. "It is so wonderful here," she said. "But how do you manage to have such freedom? I mean, every night you walk in the gardens, you work, the youngsters play. I don't understand how you can be so free in a building used by humans each day."

"That is the wonder of it," old Mr. Baxter said. "Thanks to the colonel here, we have a tightly run community. By day we live underground and by night overground until the humans' night cleaning crew comes."

The colonel, a broad-shouldered mouse whose graying whiskers turned slightly upward, touched a napkin to his mouth. "Yes, and we are quite strict about enforcing the rules, madam, as you already know. No mice allowed overground before the 11:00 p.m. all clear. All mice must be underground when curfew sounds at 1:00 a.m. Saturdays, and Sundays curfew is normally extended until 3:00 a.m. if so ordered by the head of curfew control." He paused before adding. "At no time is anyone allowed past the first floor gardens into any of the upper floors—a law strictly enforced by our patrols."

At the colonel's last words, Horace swallowed the large piece of tart in his mouth, nearly choking on it.

"You okay, mate?" Max whispered, patting Horace's back. Horace managed a nod.

Leta was asking the colonel a question. "But how can you be sure no humans will show up when you least expect them?" she said. Every eye including Horace's turned to the colonel.

He smiled. "My dear, for many, many years we have carefully plotted the comings and goings of the humans in this building. We have charts and maps of every floor top to bottom, made at great risk when the community first opened. Our patrols are trained to report any changes however small. No one is allowed overground into the gardens if the patrols have the slightest reason to suspect anything unusual going on among the humans." He paused and took a sip of tea. "We have also learned some of the humans' means of communication. I am pleased with our sophisticated system at present, and of course, with our excellent patrols."

Horace hoped for a chance to talk privately to Leta or her aunt, but the two were quickly surrounded by others eager to greet them. He and Max left quietly. The colonel's words, *No one is ever allowed above the first floor gardens,* had nearly made him choke. He and Max would cross that very border onto the second floor tonight. To be caught meant certain arrest and probably exile or worse. Horace glanced at Max. "We're still on for tonight?" he asked.

Max nodded. "I'll be there," he said. "Though for the life of me, I don't know why I put up with risking both our necks."

"You're the best, Max. It won't be much longer," Horace promised. He knew the danger was real. The whole thing had to be kept strictly a secret between them, but he was almost finished. There was still an hour before overground hours would begin when he left Max at the west tunnel, still enough time for him to change and fill his backpack.

At eleven sharp Horace hurried to join Max at their meeting place, a spot high on the garden slope and hidden from the sight of anyone in the lower gardens by a heavy growth of feather ferns. The smell of night-blooming flowers floated upward to him. Below him the grand dining room of the Fleur Gardens Restaurant gleamed in cold moonlight shining through the glass walls and casting shadows on white tablecloths and cushioned chairs. Lost in thought he jumped when Max touched him.

"Well, mate, time to go," Max said. Horace nodded, and together the two made their way along a little used path that wound close towards the north edge, where the garden bordered a wide stairway. The high steep slopes here were usually deserted. When an abrupt turn took them headlong into a bent figure, Horace backed straight into Max.

It was Leta. She looked at them from under long dark lashes, her black eyes sparkling. "Horace isn't it, and am I right this is Max?" She extended a dainty paw which Max shook with his large one. Looking at Horace, she said, "I saw you leave the dinner party. Aunt Hanna tires quickly these days, so we left shortly afterwards. From your backpacks, I'd say you two are off for a hike."

Horace struggled to find his voice. "Ah, yes, we were taking an evening hike, to . . . ah . . . work up a bit of sweat." The words sounded foolish and thin to him even as he said them.

"That looks like mighty fine spearmint you've got there," Max said cheerfully. He leaned down to examine the large deeply-veined leaves that nearly filled her basket.

"I discovered this patch yesterday. Aunt Hanna likes it for her medicine stores. It makes a fine healing tea," she said, picking up her basket. "Well, I've about all I need." Her eyes turned to search Horace's face. "I suppose you like the climbing best up here where it's steepest. Do you hike often?"

"Yes, I mean, no," Horace stammered. "It has been kind of busy, but we're almost done . . . I mean practically through with fitness training," he finished lamely.

"Don't let me keep you." Leta's tone was friendly. "I really must go too. Aunt Hanna will be wondering where I am." With a whisk of her tail she was off around the bend and out of sight. Horace watched her graceful form as she appeared again where the path led to the lower gardens.

"Fitness training?" Max chided.

"Never mind. Let's get on with it," Horace said. The old feeling in the pit of his stomach came as he turned with Max toward the north garden border. Whenever he and Max crossed the border, he knew not even Mr. Baxter would understand. Everything beyond the border, all eleven floors of the building, was forbidden territory. Max's sturdy back with its heavy pack pushed through the thicket ahead, and Horace quickened his pace. Under his fur he felt the broken ivory tree swing against his neck.

As they reached the last stone terrace that marked the end of the sloping gardens and the first floor of offices, Max signaled for Horace to fall back. Crouching down in a patch of broad leaves and pulling Horace with him, he whispered, "Patrol."

Just beyond the stone wall, four large gray mice wearing the badges of the patrol marched swiftly across the landing above the grand staircase. "Border check," Horace whispered. "And isn't that Barga leading them?"

Even from this distance he could see the shiny new patrol leader's stripes on Barga's uniform sash. A border arrest would be a feather in his cap.

As if reading his mind, Max said, "So long as we're on this side of the garden border, we're safe. But it won't do to have Barga get suspicious and start tailing us."

Horace swallowed hard. Each time he and Max made their way to the architect's office on the second floor, a voice inside tugged at him reminding him they were breaking the law. "But," he told himself, "Max and I are careful to be back before curfew." Besides, they were almost finished, and one day he'd share his work with the world.

Barga and his patrol reappeared, marched swiftly down the stairs, and disappeared into the restaurant below. Horace stepped cautiously back onto the path. In one jump they were both over the ledge and running lightly along the carpeted hallway of the second floor. The security night-lights cast shadows on the walls giving the deserted hallway the look of a long cave. On each side were several doors to offices.

"It always gives me the shivers," Horace said, "to see all those closed doors."

Max shifted his pack and nodded. "I don't know, mate. I'd a good sight rather have them closed than open and us passing by right in sight of some human."

The ends of Horace's whiskers quivered as always when he thought of danger. Of course no humans were around at this time of night. "Cheer up, Max, so long as we're back before curfew we'll be out of the office before any of the humans' cleaning crew reaches this floor," he said glancing behind him.

"Here we go," Max whispered, as they came to a halt in front of the last doorway on the left of the long hallway.

 **CHAPTER 3**

Standing in front of the closed office door, Max gave a low whistle. As Horace watched, he opened his pack and removed a small climbing rope with a hook attached at one end. "Stay back now," Max ordered. The grapple worked smoothly, its edge catching fast to the mail slot partway up the smooth wooden door. Max held the rope tightly while Horace climbed to its top and perched on the ledge of the mail slot. It was a lot easier than jumping up.

Behind him Max breathed heavily as he climbed. "If you just wouldn't eat so many of Miss Bea's pies," Horace teased, "you wouldn't sound like you'd just swum the creek in flood time."

Grinning, Max continued to pull himself up the rope. "You know we have to show our appreciation for all the fair mousels, and I do my best," he said. Horace moved to make room for him while Max drew the rope up and dropped it through to the inside of the office. In a few minutes both were on the soft, carpeted floor of the architect firm of Pearson and Stump. They hurried past the reception desk to the inner offices where desks and drawing tables, each in its own cubicle, filled the long room. Horace and Max went straight to number three. While Max scurried to the desk lamp and turned it on, Horace quickly brought out supplies from his backpack and laid them on an empty corner of the desk top.

Max turned the swivel lamp so that its light shone directly on the wall. Slowly, and with a painful throb in his throat, Horace took in the wonders before him. Paintings of mountains, rivers, forests, city skyscrapers, and strange landscapes filled the wall with scenes from the outside world.

"Every time I see that look on your face," Max said, "I get a strange feeling that coming up here so you can paint has to be right even if it means trouble ahead." He wiggled his whiskers and sniffed. "Almost overcomes me watching you. Who ever heard of such a thing as a mouse who can draw pictures as fine as a human's? No one has ever done such a thing before, mate."

Horace threw a grateful look at his friend. "Couldn't have done it without you, old buddy." Horace had discovered that he was an artist from the first night when he and Max had come upon the paintings and a piece of an old charcoal pencil. Horace had begun to draw one of the paintings on a bit of scrap paper. The wonder was that his paws seemed to know just what to do, and before long he was sketching away. And it was good! The colonel might banish him from the community and would probably banish Max with him if they were caught past the first-floor boundary, but he couldn't help himself. He had to copy them all. Back in his quarters, hidden behind a curtain his paintings lined the wall. He had learned to mix colors and use a brush and now the pictures were almost ready for the day he would bring them all out in a grand showing for the mice of Fleur Gardens. After tonight only one picture remained to be copied.

With a small bit of shaved charcoal pencil that Max had rescued from a wastebasket, Horace began sketching a woodland scene. Something about it stirred him. What was it Mr. Baxter had said? The brother he didn't know he had until now might be living in some woodland place, if he had survived! He worked silently and swiftly filling in the scrap of drawing paper.

"Snack time," Max announced half an hour later. On the desktop, his backpack bulged with bits of pencil, paper, rubber bands, even a clip he'd found in the wastebaskets while Horace worked on his drawing. The nameplate on the desk said *Dave Billings*. It was his wastebasket that always held the remains of a brown bag lunch. Tonight the bag produced a chunk of good roll and crumbs of thick yellow cheese. As they ate, Horace looked at the picture of a little girl in a metal frame near the calendar. He supposed it was Billings's little girl.

They finished their lunch, and Max burped appreciatively. "Time to read the desk calendar," he reminded Horace.

Horace climbed onto the edge of the open page, peered at the words, and read aloud, "Pride goes before a fall."

"Well, mate," Max said, "That's something to watch out for."

Horace laughed as he went back to work on his sketch. For all his strength and skill, Max was one of the humblest mice Horace knew.

He was just finishing a final touch to the corner of the picture when Max announced, "Time's up," and pointed to the large clock over Billings's desk. Horace nodded, carefully rolled his sketch, and placed it inside his pack. Holding his pack with one paw, he reached for a stick of charcoal with the other, but it rolled and fell from the desk top onto the floor. Without thinking Horace jumped for it and crash landed directly onto the stick, splintering it into pieces. Quickly he picked up what he could and started after Max who was already hooking the climbing rope to the mail slot. Horace reached the rope just as Max uttered a startled, "Oh no, mate! You've left tracks plain as can be for anyone to see."

Turning to look, Horace saw a set of mice tracks in perfect black charcoal dust leading straight from the desk to the office door. "I must have gotten the dust on my paws when I jumped. I can't leave them like that."

Mouse tracks would mean one thing to the cleaning lady—a call to maintenance for the exterminators. The idea of humans hunting down and killing mice brought a deep chill inside him. It could mean the end of the Fleur Garden Mice.

From his backpack Max took a large cloth and tore it in two. Working together, the two of them lifted and blew and wiped up the dust bit by bit, careful not to rub the black marks from Horace's feet deeper into the carpet. When at last they were through, the signs of mice tracks were gone, though here and there dark smudges dotted the carpeting. "Well, it will do," Horace said. "No one could take those for tracks."

Max grunted, then straightened and stared at the clock. "Oh, oh," he said, "We could be running into Barga's patrol if it gets any later." It had taken so long to clean away Horace's tracks that curfew was almost upon them.

"Don't worry, we'll make it," Horace assured him. A worse thought had suddenly sent his stomach into a knot. They could hide in the gardens below, but not up here! The cleaning women entered the building through a back entrance directly to the elevators leading to the second floor and above. At any minute one of the women could arrive at this office.

CHAPTER 4

Minutes later they were running swiftly down the hall to the stairway. Horace didn't stop until they'd reached the landing above the grand staircase. Sweet scents of night-blooming flowers rose from the garden. "Hey, where is everybody?" he whispered peering below. The gardens were deserted, and with a sinking heart Horace looked at Max. "Curfew," he whispered. "We've missed the curfew."

"It was all that cleanup that did it," Max said. He thumped his paw heavily against a railing. "Now what do we do?" Horace was about to say something when Max quickly crouched low. "Get down; it's a patrol."

"Barga," Horace muttered. Peering between the railings of the staircase, he watched Barga and his men hurrying up one of the garden paths. They were heading toward the tunnel that led in one direction to Max's place and in the other to Horace's.

"They're patrolling the tunnels," Max groaned. "Barga must be trying to impress the captain. They don't usually start checking the tunnels this early. There goes a good cup of hot tea and a night's sleep."

"My fault," Horace said. "I never should have gotten you into this." His whiskers drooped.

"You didn't make me go." Max gave Horace a stern look. "We're in this together, but don't for a minute think I like it."

Horace hid a grin. "Thanks." He turned to look quickly behind him. "One thing's for sure; we can't stay here. Any time now the cleaning crew will be coming to do this floor and the restaurant and the staircase we're sitting on! If one of them sees us, you know what that could mean." His whiskers tingled at the thought. Here on the exposed staircase, the danger of being seen was only a tail behind them. Without another word Horace leaped for the terrace ledge and landed in a bed of broad-leafed hostas. Max tumbled in right behind him.

"A fine fix," Max muttered. "We can't go into our tunnel now that Barga and his men are there. We'll have to wait until the patrols move on. Meanwhile, we have to stay clear of humans."

Horace nodded. He was tired and miserable. "Maybe we better separate. If any of the gardeners show up, just stay as far away from them as you can."

Max interrupted. "I don't know, mate. I think we'd do better to stay together. That way if one of us dozes off, the other one can wake him up if there's trouble. We'll need to be well hidden, but close enough to slip inside when the time comes." He yawned widely.

Horace's mind raced. They were both tired, so it might be better to stay together. "Well, if you think so, Max," he said. He was about to say something more when suddenly the underground irrigation system went off.

Geysers of water rose all about them and fell in sheets drenching them where they crouched. Horace gasped at the shock and brushed the bitter stuff from his mouth. Bitter? The water was bitter!

"Chemicals," Max sputtered. "They've mixed something with the water. Come on, we've got to get out of here." Spray from the fountains of poisoned water rising and falling everywhere cut off vision so that Horace could barely see ahead of him. Max had a grip on his shoulder and was pulling him along. "The nearest tunnel, mate, in the palms," Max yelled. Somehow Max reached the palms, and once under the shelter of their broad leaves, they slid and slipped into the small hidden entrance at the base of a thick plant.

Inside the tunnel Horace leaned against the wall and breathed deeply. Max rubbed his face and then his fur. Horace wiped the stinging water from his eyes. "That was close," he whispered.

As his eyes adjusted to the dim light, Horace saw that every door in the tunnel was closed for the night. The tunnel was far removed from their own. They were safe for the moment, but what about the patrol? Barga and his men would check every tunnel at least once, going from one tunnel to the next by means of the small connecting tunnels. "Now what do we do?" he whispered. "We were safer outside. If Barga comes along, there's no place in here to hide."

"A little while longer out in that rain, and they'd be carrying us away," Max said. "That stuff may be meant for insects, but too much is deadly. We'll just have to wait here and hope it clears up soon so we can take our chances out there." Max slumped down against the wall.

Inside, Horace felt himself slump. By morning the poison would have lost its strength to affect mice, but what now? If they were caught here after curfew, not even in their own tunnel, Barga would no doubt arrest them. And what of the colonel? He didn't want to think. He had been stooped over but shot up straight, his heart racing, as one of the doors in the tunnel opened. Wrapped in an old dressing gown, a small figure carrying a basket on her arm hurried toward them. Her head was down as if she were lost in thought, and she didn't see them until she was almost upon them. She gasped and stepped back. It was Leta's Aunt Hanna.

"Please don't be alarmed," Horace said quickly. "It's just Max and me. We were caught out after curfew, and I'm afraid the sprinklers went on, only they're spraying chemicals tonight. And, ah . . . well, with the curfew law, and the sprinklers and all, we came in here just till it's safe." He knew he wasn't explaining very well by the look of utter surprise on her face.

Max tried to help. "Sorry if we frightened you, Aunt Hanna. Our own quarters are in the west tunnels, but the patrols are in the tunnels and won't be pleased to find us here or anywhere out after curfew. We'll be going just as soon as the sprinklers turn off."

All three of them turned as a sleepy voice behind them said, "Aunt Hanna, are you all right?" It was Leta, and as she appeared in the open doorway, she gave a small cry.

"Hush, child," Aunt Hanna said softly. "Just late visitors. Come," Aunt Hanna commanded, gesturing for Max and Horace to follow her. Quickly she shooed them all inside the door and shut it tightly for the night. "I was going to leave this basket of fresh bread and seeds at the widow Jem's door, but that can wait till tomorrow."

Leta drew her robe more firmly about her and stared at Horace and Max. "And to what do we owe this unexpected pleasure?" she asked in a voice not at all happy. Her small nose wrinkled at the unpleasant odor of the chemicals Horace and Max carried into the room.

"Caught out after curfew, my dear," Aunt Hanna said. "And it looks as though there is nowhere they can go at the moment. I believe we shall have to shelter these two for now. After you've dried off, you may sleep in the kitchen," she said nodding towards a small room to her left. "It won't be as comfortable as you are used to, but there are extra blankets and at least you will be warm enough. I'll fetch towels." She disappeared into another room leaving Leta still standing there, staring at Max and Horace.

Horace felt his whiskers twitching. He could barely think what to say. "Sorry to trouble you like this. We were out and somehow didn't notice how late it was getting. But the colonel is pretty strict about rules, and it would mean trouble to run into a patrol after curfew. Course it's a good thing for all of us, the rules I mean." He couldn't seem to stop his flow of words. "Anyway, things didn't go as usual." He stopped abruptly. He'd as much as said they had done this kind of thing before.

Leta smiled and looked questioningly at Horace then at Max. "Yes, I remember you were both on your way to exercise earlier this evening. You must be quite dedicated. Now, if you will excuse me, I'll help prepare your pallets." She brushed past them into the kitchen.

Horace felt miserable as he turned to Max. "She doesn't believe me," he said.

Max grinned. "Buck up, mate. We can bunk here for the night, and tomorrow we'll be back in our own place." He looked smug. "Now that Aunt Hanna, she's one fine mouse, she is. More than likely anyone else would have been scared out of their wits, too scared to lend a hand."

Leta said little as she showed them into the kitchen quarters. After she left, Horace rubbed down his fur and lent a paw to Max. At last, lying on his pallet, Horace drew a deep breath of relief and pulled the blanket up to his whiskers.

No sounds came from outside the thick walls of the nest. The kitchen still smelled faintly of fresh baked bread and apple stew. Horace thought about the first night he had seen Leta and her aunt half-covered with snow. What had it been like for them out in the world? Their home had been destroyed by rats, everything gone. Well, at least they were safe now. He turned over on his side. He pulled the covers closer. Max was already snoring lightly, and his own eyes were closing.

Horace opened his eyes. Max was shaking his shoulder. He squeezed his eyes shut, and then quickly opened them again. Max was already dressed. The sand clock on the wall above him marked the hour as dawn. Slowly the events of the night before came to him. They'd spent the night in old Aunt Hanna's kitchen. Quickly he threw back his blanket. "We'd better get out of here before the whole world comes awake."

Quietly Horace rolled his straw-stuffed pallet next to Max's in a corner of the little kitchen. On a wooden table near the sand pit, a bowl of bread dough from the night before waited for the morning baking. Bright towels hung on pegs, and above them bundles of drying herbs dangled, giving off a sweet smell that tickled Horace's nose. There was no sign that Leta or her aunt were up yet. Closing the door softly behind him, Horace felt the cool air of the tunnel against his face as he joined Max.

CHAPTER 5

From behind one of the closed doors, the smell of freshly baked bread drifted into the deserted tunnel. Horace sniffed deeply and hurried after Max. When they reached the east tunnel, Max waved a paw silently before turning away toward his quarters. Horace nodded back and with a sigh of relief headed to his own door.

As he laid his pack on a small work table, the easel Max had made from bits of old tunnel wood caught his eye. Breakfast was forgotten. He drew out last night's rolled up picture from his backpack. He placed it on the easel, uncovered his paints, and began to mix them. First he stirred the red of wine berries, then dandelion yellow, nut browns, and finally leaf tints boiled with nightshade. Under his brush strokes, trees came into glowing color, their leaves lifted in the wind. Below the trees he had sketched in a river, and soon it flowed over rocks in gleaming ripples and splashed against a small sandy beach. At last Horace was satisfied. Carefully he washed his brushes, put away his paints, and drew the curtain that hid his bedroom studio.

Yawning mightily, he glanced at the sand clock. It was almost time to report to work at the west tunnels. Hastily he packed a lunch of bread and seeds into his pack, then fixed himself a breakfast of nut bread, apple, and tea.

In the crowded tunnel Horace nodded to neighbors going about their business. The tunnel narrowed where it joined a short connecting branch, slowing the steady stream of mice moving through it and forcing Horace to keep well to the wall. Though he was one of the youngest mice on the tunnel crew, Horace already felt a deep pride for the system. Anyone could travel throughout the entire community without going into the overground gardens. As he neared the west gate, he saw Max already at the work site.

By supper time a minor break in the west tunnel wall gleamed with a new seal coat and fresh support beams. "That's it," Horace said. He grinned at Max as they headed home. Dirt streaked Max's face. Horace wiped at his own only to see a muddy mess across his paw.

"Nothing like a good day's work, mate, to give a fellow an appetite," Max said patting his ample stomach.

"Can't think why you didn't become a chef, Max, or a gleaner," Horace waved a muddy paw. "Think of it—all you wanted to eat and no cave-ins, no dirt."

Max grinned. "And yourself, mate, you'd make a fine fellow for the night patrol. Blend right in with the shadows with all that mud you're wearing."

"No thanks," Horace said. The thought of being part of a patrol under Barga's command irked him. "It's not my cup of tea," he added.

Max put his canteen to his mouth and drank deeply. "Nothing like good water to clear the throat of all that dust," he said, "and we've got plenty of dust. The trouble with these tunnels is they're old, but there's no more ground in the gardens that can be safely tunneled. Which means," continued Max, "that with all the growing families around here, the colonel will have to make some changes soon." Max put away his canteen and looked at Horace. "Might be some could start a second Fleur Gardens community. There's always a few ready to try a new life out there."

Horace thought of the forest painting he'd finished that morning. "Max, it's a big world out there, but do you really think that somewhere another place like this could exist?"

"Can't rightly say, mate," Max said. "It's a good life here, no cats, no traps, and plenty of holidays, feasts, good friends, and Mr. Baxter's stories. Don't suppose there's many left who know the traditions and stories the way he does."

Horace's thoughts drifted back to the woodland painting hidden in his bedroom. A place like that would be wild, mysterious, and dangerous. He shook his head to clear it. Was it possible he had a brother somewhere out there? "Anyway," he said, "winter is no time for a journey. Whatever the colonel's plans are, they'll have to wait until spring." Horace glanced at Max. "For now, I want to finish the paintings."

Max cleared his throat. "Well, mate, we best get on with it before the holidays set in. I'll see you overground—same place, same time tonight," he said as he turned towards his own nest.

"Tonight then," Horace called. Christmas Eve was nearly upon them and the grand feast. Every mouse in Fleur Gardens who could lift a paw would be helping with the great yearly celebration.

Nightfall came swiftly. When Horace rounded the path to the usual meeting place near the deserted north border, Max stepped from behind a giant fern. They reached the architect's office and were soon inside. Horace set up his drawing and began sketching.

Behind him Max rummaged through the wastebasket looking for leftovers. "Not a thing," he grumbled climbing out.

"Mm," Horace murmured, continuing to draw a thin line of shadow on his canvas.

Max shook his head and muttered, "Useless talking to myself." It was not until much later when Horace finally stopped for a break that Max got his attention. "No lunch, mate," he said. "I happen to have a few seeds in my pack." He laid them out on the desk top. "From the looks of things, I'm guessing Dave didn't come to work today, and that explains why there's no bag lunch," Max said aloud.

Horace looked around at the desk top. There were no fresh memos on the desk, nothing to show that Dave Billings had been there. Curious, he looked at the desk calendar. From his perch on the open page he called, "No one has turned the page since we were here last." Though they had never met and never would, Horace had a fondness for the man they knew as Dave. He liked the way he doodled on his memo pad, liked the picture of the little girl on his desk, and the sort of comfortable way he left things he was working on lying around. "Well, if he's home sick, I hope it won't be for too long." He looked at the large wall clock and then at Max, who yawned widely. "Max, old man, why don't we call it a night. We've both been going at this pretty hard, and I'm sure I can finish this sketch from memory in the morning."

The look of relief that swept over Max's face took away any faint regrets Horace felt as he swiftly put away his working tools. It was early enough that they should have no trouble slipping back into the gardens to join the nightly gatherings.

Keeping low, Horace led the way across the small open area between the hall and the garden wall. The thick growth of fern and hosta made good cover along the stone terrace, and the two were soon safely back in the gardens. With a hearty "good night," Max left to make his way toward the lower terraces. Horace smiled as he watched Max turn toward Miss Bea's small garden plot. Horace had only one thing in mind, his own nest, and he hurried towards the path. He nearly jumped when a soft voice said, "Why, Horace, out hiking again?" He felt his face warming as he turned to see Leta's small figure straighten up from a patch of thyme. She brushed her paws and picked up her basket.

"I, ah . . . I've been meaning to thank you for your hospitality," he said.

Leta smiled. "It's not me you want to thank. Aunt Hanna is the one who takes in strays, and other sorts," she added.

"Sorry, it won't happen again. It was careless of me. My fault really."

Leta shifted her basket to her arm. Her eyes snapped as she said, "You must be turning over a new leaf, or at least Max seems to be. I saw him heading towards Miss Bea's." She raised her eyes. "And have you learned your lesson as well?"

"Yes, Max is a good teacher." Horace's heart raced. "May I take your basket? I happen to know where to find a small hidden patch of rosemary that your aunt might like to know about."

"Rosemary? Are you sure? Aunt Hanna uses the leaves to make her ointment for sore muscles. The tea is good for headaches too, but we haven't seen a bit of rosemary here." She handed him the basket. "I'd be obliged if you'd show me the patch."

Horace had seen the rosemary close to the north border of the garden. He hoped it was still there. It was. It's long, thin leaves glistened bright green and healthy. He knelt by Leta and helped her fill her basket.

"That ought to make Aunt Hanna happy," Leta said, brushing away damp earth from her knees as she rose.

The smell of the rosemary made Horace think of tea, and suddenly he found himself saying, "Leta, I don't know about you, but I could go for a cold cherry-mint tea right now. Let me introduce you to the best cherry-mint stand around here. Of course, it's the *only* one." He picked up her basket and held out his arm.

"I'd like that," Leta said simply, taking his arm. "There's so much here in Fleur Gardens that Aunt Hanna and I never dreamed of before. It's like," she hesitated, "I can't find the right word . . . sort of like being in a whole new world, I guess." For the next half-hour Horace forgot everything else as they drank their cherry-mints and talked of plants and teas and the wonders of life in Fleur Gardens.

They were standing near the great dining room when curfew sounded. Horace was about to ask if he might escort Leta to the Christmas Eve feast when Barga strode into sight, headed directly for them.

Barga's new gold stripes gleamed on the shoulders of his patrol sash. The hilt of his weapon flashed above his waistband. He ignored Horace. "Curfew, Miss Leta. May I show you to your tunnel?" Without waiting for an answer, he took Leta's arm firmly. "Isn't your tunnel in the opposite direction, Horace?" he said. "You'd better be on your way." His look at Horace was smug. "Orders are orders, you know, and curfew is in effect as of now."

Horace turned to Leta. Her eyes were wide with surprise. "I guess I'll be going then," he said.

"It's been fun. Thank you," Leta called over her shoulder. Barga was already leading her away.

"We'll do it again," Horace shouted, then stopped. He had almost said tomorrow night. "Sometime soon, that is," he finished under his breath. He felt suddenly tired. He and Max already had their plans for tomorrow night. What would Leta think if she knew they had not only broken the curfew the other night, but night after night they broke the community's strictest law? Were the paintings worth it? Was the risk too high? How could he ever tell where his ideas for the paintings had come from? The colonel would banish both him and Max from Fleur Gardens. If his mother and brother were still alive, they would never be welcome to the Gardens if the colonel banished him. With a sigh he headed toward the nearest tunnel. Only a few more nights and he'd be finished. After that . . . well, he wouldn't think about it now. Surely a law, even a good one, shouldn't stand in the way of doing something great. Still, he would be glad when he and Max no longer needed to visit the second floor.

He took the nearest tunnel entrance and hurried down it to the connecting tunnel that led to his own. Horace's place was not far from the gate that led outside the building. He was already thinking of the colors he would need for the painting in his pack when the cries of angry voices and clashing metal directly ahead of him chased everything else from his mind. The gate! Horace froze. An attack!

Rats were attacking the patrol at the main gate! Without thinking Horace ran to help. Ahead of him the gate stood wide open, and not three feet from it one of the outdoor patrols was fighting off several large rats. Horace could see the patrol advancing slowly as the rats retreated. The colonel's mice, well-trained and armed with steel weapons, moved forward pushing the rats well

away from the gate. Unarmed as he was, Horace knew he could do little to help. As he watched, a sudden blur of dark movement near the gate made him gasp in horror.

Large black rats swept through the gate! It was a trick! Horace cried out a warning. "Behind you, Captain! They're coming into the tunnel. It's a trap," he screamed. In an instant part of the patrol turned back. Above the chaos and clashing sounds, Horace heard the battle alarm calling all patrols to the gate.

But he had no time to think at all as a large black rat, with gleaming angry eyes and teeth bared, knocked him to the dirt floor. Horace shoved against the hairy chest of his attacker with all his might. The rat's teeth snapped just inches from his throat. Horace wrenched his body under the rat's hold, turning his head just as the fangs sank into his shoulder.

CHAPTER 6

Blinding pain seared Horace's shoulder as a mountain of foul darkness pressed down on him. He couldn't breathe. The smothering blackness turned into flashing lights and hot knives that tore his shoulder as the rat's body lifted violently, loosening its hold on Horace and rolling onto its side. Horace gulped air and groaned.

"Are you all right?" a deep voice asked. One of the patrol, holding his weapon in his paw, leaned over him. Horace couldn't remember the fellow's name.

"Just winded," Horace answered weakly, his gaze turning to where the rat's body lay. It shook violently twice, stiffened, and was still.

"Good. Get your shoulder tended to, and take shelter quickly," the guard commanded. Holding his weapon high he dashed off towards the gate leaving Horace lying where he was. Horace lay on the ground staring at the dead rat. Just beyond it, a little further up the tunnel, he saw the bodies of three other rats. He tried to remember how many had entered the tunnel, but all he could picture were the huge dark shapes pounding through the gate. Near the gate, the clash of steel and cries of battle were fierce. When he moved to sit, pain roared through his shoulder and a wave of dizziness hit him. He shut his eyes to keep the tunnel from spinning. When he opened them again, he saw that the front of him was covered with blood. Carefully he touched his left shoulder where a deep burning had set in. His paw came away wet with blood. So it was his own blood all over him. Holding his paw to the wound in his shoulder, he pushed himself onto his right side. He could see the gate just as two of the patrol closed it behind them. Horace winced knowing that some would pay with their lives in this battle. He shut his eyes. When he opened them, the noise of fighting sounded further away. He lay still and listened. Like most wild animals, the rats wouldn't fight in an open exposed place such as the road beyond the building. Horace shivered and listened once more, but this time he was certain the fighting was distant. *Once the rats are really on the run, they'll head for the woods*, he told himself. That fact would give the patrols a chance to follow the road to the north gate to safety.

The light footsteps of someone running towards him made Horace try to sit up again. Once more his head swayed and his vision blurred. Pain seared his shoulder down into his arm. Beside him a small figure knelt and reached to touch him. "Why, Horace, you're hurt." Leta's voice was the last thing Horace had expected.

"What are you doing here? You ought not to be here," he said gruffly. The gate was closed, and though it seemed safe enough for the moment, the bodies of the dead rats around them were a grisly sight.

Leta took off her shawl and placed it over his shoulder. "Aunt Hanna wanted you to have her recipe for rosemary tea. Then I heard the alarm. I didn't know what to do." Her voice quavered. "I just kept coming, and then I saw you." She kept on winding the shawl over and under his arm. "There," she said, "that will hold for now."

"Thanks," Horace said through gritted teeth. "We need to get out of here." Still gritting his teeth and holding a paw to his wounded shoulder, he pushed himself to his feet. Leta reached out to steady him. A strange light-headedness filled him, and his legs wobbled. "I could use an arm," he said grimly. "My place isn't far, but I don't seem to have any strength." He swayed dangerously as Leta draped his good arm about her shoulders. His weight sagged heavily against her.

By the time they reached his door, Horace had the feeling that his body was somehow moving along without any help from him. Curious, he looked at Leta whose face seemed to be far away and fading by the moment.

"Oh, dear," Horace heard her say as he sank against her arm and dropped like a stone to the floor. When Horace opened his eyes, he was lying on the floor in his own sitting room. Leta bent over him with a pillow and tucked it around his shoulder. "Are you in much pain?" she asked.

Horace gritted his teeth. "Not so bad," he said. His head ached and his shoulder and arm burned, but as long as he didn't move them, he could bear it. A shiver shook him, and he groaned.

"You're cold," Leta cried. She left him and returned with a blanket. "That's a nasty wound. It's still bleeding some," she said as she spread the blanket over him. "I'll fetch clean towels before I go for help." While Leta packed his shoulder with the towels, Horace tried to fight off his dizziness but gave up. He closed his eyes hoping it would go away. He opened them once to see Leta's face close to his and closed them again.

Suddenly Leta jumped and let out a cry. Startled, Horace opened his eyes wide. "Oh, Max," she said, "you gave me a start."

It is all right, Horace thought, closing his eyes again. *Max is here.*

"What's happened? Mate? Wake up now, old fellow," Horace opened his eyes and tried to smile. Max pulled the blanket away from the soaked towels. "Where did you get this?" he asked.

"Rats," Horace said and closed his eyes again.

"I found him in the main tunnel, a bit dazed from his wound," Leta said. "There was a dead rat nearby. Several of them." She paled at the memory. "We came this far before he fainted. Will he be all right?"

As Max unwrapped Leta's shawl from his shoulder, Horace turned his head slightly to look. Large jagged teeth marks had torn the flesh almost to the bone. "Ugly," he said.

"We need linen, towels, anything to press against it and stop the bleeding" Max ordered.

Leta ran off and returned with cloths and more towels.

Max applied steady pressure. The bleeding seemed to be stopping. "That's good," he said. Horace's eyes fluttered once and closed again. Carefully Max ran his paws over Horace's head. "Ah, just as I thought. There's a knob the size of a pea here on the back of your head. You must have struck your head when you fell, and what with the loss of blood and a possible concussion, it's no wonder you passed out."

As Max spoke, Horace opened his eyes. "It needs stitches, right Max?" he asked in a faint voice.

"Yes, of course, mate." Max leaned over him. "From the looks of you, that shoulder will need a lot of stitches and a good cleaning out. Nothing like rat wounds to bring on an infection."

Horace made a movement to lift himself and groaned. "I feel like someone hit me over the head with a brick." He lay back and closed his eyes. He opened them again quickly and asked, "Max? The battle? Is it over?"

"The battle is over, thankfully. I came to see what news you might have had about the rat break-in. I'd no idea you'd been hurt. I better be going for one of the healers. Miss Leta, you'll have to keep pressure on this wound, but I'll be back in a wink." Max stood up to go.

Leta bent to press her paws on the towels covering the wound. "If it's a healer you need, Max, Aunt Hanna is the best. She'll know what to do, and it won't be the first time she's sewn up a wound. Please let me run for her."

"Well now, Miss Leta, that would be fine except that I'd not like to see you alone in the tunnels until the whole place has been thoroughly searched. It's not likely, but with a break-in like this one, we can't be too careful. I'll go and fetch Aunt Hanna, if you'll stay here with our patient. And this time, better keep the door shut and barred." Max suddenly strode to the open curtain to the bedroom and pulled it shut. Leta looked at him, her eyes wide with surprise. Max gestured toward the closed curtain. "This is not the time to explain, but if you've been in there then you know about the paintings." Leta nodded. Max cleared his throat. "Well, then, I'll need to ask a favor of you. No one else knows about the paintings yet, and we'd like to keep it that way for now. Horace?" he looked questioningly at Horace.

"I can explain everything," Horace said in a low, weak voice. "I'd like to do that when this head settles down to normal again, if that's all right with you?" A shadow of pain crossed his face.

Leta put a paw to her throat. "Yes, of course," she promised.

"Good," Max said. "Then the sooner I get your aunt, the better."

Leta saw Max to the door, and then kneeling by Horace she again applied pressure to the wound. Horace opened his eyes to look at her. "About the pictures," he said, his voice squeaking with exhaustion.

"Hush now," Leta interrupted. "Your secret is safe with me. Sometime when you're ready, we'll talk."

Horace felt bone weary, his mouth dry. "Please, I think I'd like something to drink. There's tea in the kitchen warming pit," he managed to say.

A small frown wrinkled Leta's forehead. "I suppose that would be all right" she said. Carefully she stopped applying pressure to Horace's shoulder, watched for any sudden gush of blood, and seeing none, hurried into the kitchen. Hot stones buried in packed sand kept a small kettle of tea warm all day. It was an old mouse custom.

Leta brought the tea in a saucer. Gently she lifted Horace's head to rest against her lap while he drank. "Do you mind," she said, "if I ask you one thing?" Without waiting for an answer, she went on. "Are all those paintings back in there yours? I mean did you do them?"

Horace's eyes grew wide, and he stopped drinking the tea. "Yes, all of them. But it's a long story." He sighed, closed his eyes, and opened them again.

"I shouldn't have asked. Not another word," she commanded holding his tea close so that he could drink it.

CHAPTER 7

Horace felt a lazy warmth steal over him from the aromatic herbal mixture Aunt Hanna had given him. Talking to him in a gentle voice, she began to stitch his wound. Horace gritted his teeth and tried not to move. He hoped she would be quick and was totally surprised when she said, "That should do." She placed a cool, soothing poultice on his shoulder and carefully bandaged it. "In no time you'll be fit as a fiddle," she said, covering him with a fresh blanket.

Relieved, Horace breathed deeply. "Thank you, all of you," he said. For some reason his eyes were closing. The last thing he remembered was Max saying, "Sleep well, mate."

And Horace did. For a whole day he slept, waking at last to see Max sitting in the armchair, a plate of biscuits and a cup of tea on his lap. "I think I'd like a bit of that," Horace said. His stomach felt empty and flat as a board.

"It's a good thing you finally woke up," Max called out. "I didn't know where to store all the fine cakes and custards Miss Bea and her friends brought while you slept." He patted his stomach, and Horace saw that it looked a bit fatter than usual. "I've done my best, mate, not to waste such delicacies, but there's still plenty left for you. Dinner coming right up," he said, making his way to the kitchen.

Horace groaned. "I suppose I'll just have to put up with you." He settled back against the pillow. Until the stitches were out, he had time to think and plan. While Max filled a tray in the kitchen, Horace watched his friend quietly. If his brother had lived, would he have been like Max? Sadness like a pain filled him with the sudden longing for the brother and the mother he'd never known. He imagined them coming to the gardens just as Leta had brought herself and her aunt. He pictured his brother wearing the other half of his tree necklace.

"Here you are, mate," Max said holding out a tray piled high with food that smelled as good as it looked. Horace's daydreaming vanished. He ate until he was full and once again sleepy. Leta would be back to visit soon and he had no idea what to say to her about the paintings. The sooner he finished the last picture the better, he thought as his eyes closed.

Three weeks had passed, and Horace could no longer sit still.

"I should know better," Max complained as he glared at Horace. "That arm isn't fit yet to paint with, mate."

Horace was determined. "It's not my painting arm, and besides I am feeling fine. See?" He moved his arm slowly but surely back and forth, exercising it as he'd been doing for the last two days.

"I can tell there's no arguing sense into you," Max said. "I might as well see that you don't fall into trouble."

By nightfall Horace wondered why he hadn't listened to Max.

"I told you, mate, we should have waited a few more days," Max reminded him. He reached a helping paw to Horace to lift him from the floor.

Horace gritted his teeth. A sudden spasm of pain in his shoulder, still weakened from the wound, had loosened his grip on the climbing rope. "At least the carpeting is thick. I'm all right, I think," he said. He rubbed the aching shoulder gently for a moment. "We're so close to the end of this job, I feel like nothing can stop us now."

Max had turned the light onto the next-to-last picture, and as always Horace began to study it. Like someone in a dream he opened his pack and was soon lost in his work. He barely noticed Max begin his usual rummaging in the wastebaskets until the rumbling sounds from his stomach made him aware he was hungry.

Max was sitting on the desktop next to a few broken bits of charcoal, pencil stubs, papers, a clip, and two rubber bands he'd collected. He looked at Horace. "There was no brown bag again tonight in Dave's trash can. Nothing at all in there," he said, "and the calendar hasn't been changed since the last time we were here."

"But that was weeks ago," Horace stood on the open desk calendar to see for himself. "You don't suppose Dave is sick? Or worse, gone for good? No, he would never leave this behind," Horace said placing a paw carefully against the glass frame of the picture of the little girl, the same picture that had been on Dave's desk all along.

Max had walked to the back edge of the desk. "I think I've discovered why Dave hasn't been in," he said in a mournful voice. "Look here."

Horace stared at a newspaper clipping tacked to the cork board above the desk. From the newspaper photo the face of the little girl in the picture on Dave's desk smiled out at them. Underneath it Horace read, "Melissa

Billings, daughter of David and Ann Billings died yesterday at United Hospital after a brief but valiant struggle with leukemia."

Horace covered his eyes with his paw. "So young," he whispered. "And Christmas is almost upon us." He felt a wave of sorrow pass over him.

Max cleared his throat. His voice was thick. "I feel like we know Dave and his wife. The way he brought his lunch so faithfully, and the things she made for him, the way he kept his little girl's picture on his desk, well, they sort of meant a loving family to me."

"Me too," Horace said. "I don't think I can do any more tonight. I'll finish this on my own in the morning." With a heavy heart he helped Max pack their things. His shoulder ached as he followed Max down the rope and back through the empty hallway. His heart was heavy for Dave and the sad loss of his little girl. He barely noticed as they passed through the long hallway of closed offices. Getting into the gardens went easily. Everyone seemed to be in the lower terraces near the great dining room. Horace searched for Leta among them, but so many mice were moving about he couldn't spot her. "Let's go on down tonight, Max," he said. "We could both use some company." Max nodded. They'd just turned a bend around a large hosta plant when he saw Leta. She was not alone. Barga stood at her side with Leta's basket on his arm.

Leta smiled. "Why Horace and Max," she said. "How are you feeling, Horace?"

"Up and about, I see," Barga said.

Horace felt his face flush. "I'm fine, thanks to your aunt's good care," he replied.

"Well, keep up the good work," Barga said. He nodded and taking Leta's arm led her down the path in the direction of the cherry stand.

Horace deliberately turned the other way. He had no intention of following Barga and Leta. "If you don't mind, Max, I think I'll take tea at home. I feel a bit tired."

Max was about to answer when a familiar voice called to them.

"I say, Horace, good to see you looking fit. And the two of you are just in time to watch us decorate the Christmas pines. Come along and tell us what you think." Mr. Baxter waved his paw towards the pine branches where Miss Bea and some of her ladies were hanging strings of red berries. Horace and Max were soon helping. At last Mr. Baxter threw a final handful of silver onto the top of a tall branch and stepped back.

"Lovely. They'll be wonderful for tomorrow night," said Miss Bea who also seemed covered with silver dust.

Mr. Baxter dusted off his paws and turned to Horace and Max. "Now that's done. You are looking well, Horace. Fit enough for a little music? I'm speaking of the Christmas Eve choir. We must have more voices. Four of our younger singers have sore throats and colds and won't be able to sing tomorrow night. I am sure you two will be a grand help."

There was nothing Horace could think of to give as an excuse. He was well enough, and of course they were free, and Mr. Baxter knew it.

"If you don't mind a squeaky alto, then I'm your man," Max said. "Come on, Horace, it will do you good."

Horace nodded. There was no escape. He only hoped they wouldn't run into Leta and Barga.

Mr. Baxter used the restaurant's smaller, private dining area for practice. For the next half-hour Horace tried to forget everything but the music and the baton in Mr. Baxter's right paw. The songs were full of joy, and as Horace sang, he felt his own heart lighten.

Christmas Eve was a time for feasting and celebrating. The mice of Fleur Gardens did both with all their hearts.

 CHAPTER 8

Christmas Eve came in all its splendor. There were no cleaning crews to worry about, no curfew. All of the offices in the building had closed the day before and would stay that way through Christmas and the day following it, as they did each Christmas holiday. Horace whistled while he handed up garlands of red seeds to Max who stood on a ladder. Miss Bea's round face beamed at Max. She was in charge and knew exactly where she wanted every decoration. The place already looked fine to Horace. In the center of the garden court, the humans had put up a large Christmas tree strung with giant colored lights. It was far too big for mouseling youngsters to enjoy. Miniature trees now lined the edge of the garden closest to the courtyard. Youngsters were everywhere, squealing with delight and getting underfoot. Horace smiled at the homemade paper chains and strings of bright rose hips that small paws tried to drape across the bottom branches of each mouseling tree. Reaching for a last sprig of holly to fix at the top, Horace handed it to Max and stepped back. "Looks like we're finished," he said. "And just in time to set up for the evening feast."

Long board tables and wooden benches filled the great court area, and the cook's helpers were busy setting places. Every table sported large bowls of red crab apples hoarded for the feast. Tall candles molded from bits of wax graced the centers. The sweet smells of mint, berry, apple, and dozens of delicate fragrances Horace couldn't even identify mingled with baking breads. The traditional dishes of roots and herbs in savory pie crusts sat covered to keep them warm on the back of the giant stove in the restaurant kitchen. For tonight, and tonight alone, the mice of Fleur Gardens had made the great kitchen their own. Each burner held a dozen mouse-sized pots, and the large oven held enough to feed an entire community, though the cooks still continued to mix and measure their Christmas specials. On one of the counters, mountains of sugar cakes filled an entire human tray borrowed for the evening. Horace directed traffic as Max carried wooden casks of Christmas punch to a table. On their last trip Max picked a couple of sweet cakes from one of the trays and gave one to Horace.

"Delicious," Horace mumbled, his mouth full of cake. Surprise warmed his face as Leta came walking out of the kitchen, her eyes merry in spite of the frown on her face.

"Better not let the widow Jem catch you stealing her cakes," she scolded then laughed. "I know they're good, because I've got one myself." She held it up and popped it into her mouth.

Horace smiled, and his thoughts raced. He hadn't expected to see Leta alone, but Barga was nowhere around. "So I guess we're all culprits," he said in a light tone. "Ah, while you have a minute, I'd like to ah, . . . I wonder if you would join me for supper?" he asked almost breathless with the effort it had taken to ask her.

Leta seemed to hesitate for a moment. "Oh," she said. "I think I've already promised to sit next to Barga. But of course there is another seat next to me on the other side, and it would be lovely if you sat there. Then I should have two companions for dinner." She smiled.

Horace's heart sank, but he couldn't refuse her invitation even if it did mean Barga would sit on one side and he on her other. "Then I'll count on it," he said. Leta hurried back into the kitchen leaving Horace staring after her.

At exactly eight o'clock the music began, and the mice of Fleur Gardens, dressed in their best finery, entered the grand court. In the dim light, candles burned brightly, silvered trees glowed, and the sight was truly breathtaking. Horace spotted Leta at about the same time Barga hurried over to her. Leta greeted them both pointing to places on her left and right and inviting them to sit. Horace looked for Max hoping he would be somewhere close, but he was several seats away next to Miss Bea. The seat next to Horace on his right was still empty.

A kindly voice asked, "May I sit by you, Horace?"

Horace looked up to see Aunt Hanna, her old face wrinkled in smiles. Relief filled him. "No one, but no one, is more welcome to sit here than you, Aunt Hanna."

Ever since she had tended his wound, visiting him twice a day to change the poultice and bringing him delicious soups and puddings, he had found her easy to talk to, and very wise. They were a third of the way through dinner before he realized he'd barely said a word to Leta. She seemed engaged in conversation with Barga, or rather, listening to Barga's tales of his escapades.

Horace turned back to Aunt Hanna. "Tell me," he said, "what it's like in the world outside our grounds. I've never been, you know, farther than the immediate grounds outside our building."

Aunt Hanna looked at him, a deep questioning in her eyes. "It was good, and it was bad," she began. Horace listened, carried away by her soft words that pictured the outside world for him. She had heard of the great fire in the city years ago that must have been the very one that brought his mother and himself to Fleur Gardens. But she knew little of the fate of those who were caught in its path.

By the time Horace felt he could eat no more, the old colonel stood to toast his friend Terra, still heavily bandaged over one eye and shoulder from the skirmish with the rats. "To a hero," the colonel cried. There were shouts of "Bravo" everywhere and the clinks of metal as some raised thimbles and others smaller vessels filled with sweet cider. Several other toasts followed, including one to the ladies of the community who had prepared the grand feast. Horace was totally unprepared to hear his name called.

"To Horace," shouted the captain of the gate patrols, "for his timely warning in the battle of the gates, a drink." Again the courtyard erupted with glad cries, and Horace felt his face grow warm. Leta smiled at him as she lifted her cup. Beside her Barga stared stonily, though he too lifted his cup.

It was time for the service to begin. With the lights dimmed and the great restaurant tree lit up, Mr. Baxter stood on a platform and spoke. His words were simple as he reminded them of past Christmases. "And now," he said raising his voice, "let us be glad this night." Shouts of "Praise be" filled the courtyard. After that the choir sang. Horace felt his heart would burst with the beauty of it all. As the song died away he remembered Dave, the architect and his little daughter Melissa. It would be a sad Christmas for Dave and his wife. A tear slid down his

face. Hastily he brushed it away in time to join the choir in a last swelling chorus.

And now the fun began. Blindfolded youngsters squealed with delight as they played the Christmas game "swat the paper cat." The lucky one to break the cat found sweet seeds pouring over him and his friends.

Outside a light snow fell, and Horace and Max joined a group of older mice for a walk. The falling snow would hide any tracks. A volunteer patrol including Barga, stood watch as some raced sleds downhill. Watching the sledders, Horace felt a sudden plop of snow on his neck and turned in time to see Leta stooping to gather more. In no time snowballs flew in all directions.

In the wee hours of Christmas Eve tired youngsters were put to bed. Horace lingered with Max and a group of friends to drink hot chocolate and munch Christmas cookies.

"A grand celebration," Mr. Baxter said as he passed them, "and a good night to you all."

Horace waved a paw. It had been a good evening.

The great hall soon emptied amidst yawns and good nights, until only he and Max were left. "Well, mate, I'm off to bed," Max said, "and you'd best be getting there yourself."

Horace nodded and followed him to the tunnels.

Morning dawned bright and cold. Horace had just finished a cup of tea and a seed cake when Max arrived. Flakes of snow glistened on Max's fur. "Come on, mate, it's Christmas," he urged. "It's still snowing lightly, and this is the one day a year we have nothing to fear from humans. The weather's perfect for sledding." Max looked hopeful, "I sort of promised to take the widow Jem's young ones sledding."

"What you want is help with those three rascals," Horace said. "Trouble follows the three of them like a second tail. You sure you're up to this, Max?"

Max pushed his new cap back on his head and grinned.

By late afternoon Horace began to feel the strain on his shoulder. The wind was growing stronger as he helped tug the homemade sled uphill. At the top of the next hill the oldest brother was busy settling Max's large sled for a ride down. Down below, Max had stopped to pick up a mitten. Horace was halfway up the hill when he heard Max yelling, "Wait for me. Don't do that. Watch out!" Too late, widow Jem's son came careening down the hill straight toward the wooden bridge that crossed a small stream. On impact the small mouse flew from the sled and disappeared under the bridge. Horace ran to help.

Under the bridge, half-buried in snow, a small round face stared up at Max and Horace. "Be grateful you didn't kill yourself," Max said, pulling the badly frightened young mouse from the heap of soft snow he'd tumbled into. "That's it for today. I think we've all had enough exercise." The youngster hung his head until Max began to laugh. "Come on, you rascal, let's get that sled," he ordered. With a surprised look in his eyes the youngster grinned.

Horace stooped to pick up a second forgotten mitten. As he bent over, a large clump of snow fell from beneath one of the wooden trusses under the bridge, and then another. He found himself staring into a dark hole. Neatly engineered beneath the truss was a tunnel—a rat tunnel from the size of it, an old one in need of repairs. *Must be an abandoned one*, he thought, but he'd report it to the captain tonight anyway.

By the time they left the widow Jem's place, helpers were beginning to take down the decorations, the tables, and all that had been so carefully put in place for the grand celebration. Horace and Max joined in the work. At last only the humans' large Christmas tree stood alone in the center of the garden court.

The snow had stopped falling and the moon risen high by the time Horace and Max headed for the tunnels. Horace handed Max a last bit of candied cherry. "I nearly forgot to tell you something curious I saw this afternoon under the bridge. From its size, it had to be an old rat tunnel," he explained as he described his find.

"So close," Max exclaimed as Horace described the rat tunnel. "How did a thing like that escape notice? The patrol likes to seal up those abandoned ones. Guess being under the bridge like that, it just wasn't spotted until now," he said.

"I suppose," Horace agreed. "I'll mention it to the captain the next time I see him."

CHAPTER 9

Monday morning Horace was at work once more on the west tunnels. As he swung his pick, his heart sang. One more picture remained. With tonight's trip, the work would be done. No more worry about breaking the law, no more being late for curfew, no more running into patrols. He whistled merrily.

Max, a little rounder and a little slower from several leftover pies of Miss Bea's, reluctantly agreed to go upstairs once more. "But this has to be the very last time," he insisted.

While the evening gardens were not yet full, they slipped away unnoticed. The architect's office looked much as it had days ago. Horace fixed his gaze on the last painting. In a black border the artist had painted a soft rose-colored sheet of musical note paper with musical bars across it. Large graceful curves swirled over the lines, and the whole page was covered from border to border with delicate feathers, tiny blue flowers, green ferns, jots of gold, and soft colors all tossing about gently as if blown by a soft breath—a song. Horace understood. The artist had captured a spring song that seemed to float heavenward. It felt so real, Horace could almost hear the notes, lovely beyond describing. Tears filled his eyes for a moment, and then he began to draw.

An hour later he heard Max muttering. "That's strange," Max said loudly. "Dave's brown bag lunch is back in the trash can again, but from the looks of it he wasn't hungry." Max had laid out the contents of the bag with care, a peanut butter sandwich with one bite missing, half a chocolate cookie, and a few crumbs. Horace munched thoughtfully on his part of the sandwich. Peanut butter happened to be a great favorite with him.

"I've never seen Dave's desk so littered," Max said. Papers were scattered about, but in a cleared space near the picture of the little girl was a single red rose bud lying on its side. Max touched it gently. "It's drying. Wonder why he didn't put it in water."

Horace felt as if his heart would break. "Looks like he left it here for her." His voice was husky. Across the room the light played gently on the painting. Horace looked at it and then at the drying rose. He had a plan. For the next half-hour he worked furiously.

"Time to go," Max announced. He had already packed.

Horace threw his things into his pack except for the drawing. With a last loving touch, he laid the mouse-sized painting on the desktop under the stem of the rose. "Coming," he said.

Max steadied the rope while Horace climbed. Then he was through the mail slot and down the other side. He rested for a moment to let the pain in his shoulder settle down. To his horror the scream of a human voice rent the air.

"A mouse, a mouse! Help, Mr. John, help." Horace turned to see a cleaning woman jumping up and down in front of the next office door. He froze. The woman, in a frenzy to escape, ran into the office she had been about to clean and slammed the door shut behind her.

Max tumbled to the hall floor, yanking the climbing rope behind him. At the sight of Max, Horace came out of his shock, and together the two ran for the stairs. With one leap they cleared the ledge and landed in the hosta beds. The unthinkable had happened!

Horace sat up, then stood shakily. Beside him, Max straightened; but before either of them could move, they were suddenly surrounded by guards, who without a word dragged them quickly into a nearby tunnel. When the entrance was shut behind them, Horace and Max found themselves face to face with Barga. His angry voice came like a dash of ice water, "What do you think you're doing? Before you say a word," Barga commanded, "I saw you both leap across the border. You are under arrest. What have you to say for yourselves?"

"Take me to the colonel," Horace said in a thin voice. "I have news for his ears only."

Barga stood his ground. "I'll give the orders here. An early curfew alarm was sounded twenty minutes ago, or didn't you two hear it? You'll report to me, and I'll decide who gets to see the colonel and when." Horace shook his head.

Max struggled between the two guards who held him firmly. "You'll get nothing from me either," he said fiercely. "It's the colonel we speak to or no one."

"We'll see about that. Take these two to the jail. No need to bother the colonel. We'll see how a few days in lockup soften their tongues." Barga put his face close to Horace's. "If you think you can't explain your actions to me, you will learn that I mean what I say—no matter how long it takes."

The guards had begun to drag Max away when Horace cried out loudly, "No. A human has seen us. There's no time to lose."

Stunned Barga stepped back. Several mice who had gathered to see what was going on cried out. Barga's face paled. "Humans? Quickly to the colonel, men. Go back to your tunnels," he commanded the small crowd around them. "Spread the word. Curfew is in force until further notice. Sound the alarm," he commanded one of the guards. "You two, come with me," he ordered Horace and Max. Horace's heart raced as they ran towards the colonel's headquarters.

The colonel, seated behind his desk, looked up with surprise at the unannounced entry of Barga and his prisoners. "What have we here, sir?" he asked.

"Humans, Colonel, these two were seen by a human," Barga blurted out.

The colonel's face paled. He stood and gripped the edge of his desk to steady himself. "Tell me," he commanded in a voice that sent a cold shiver to Horace's heart.

Horace lifted his eyes to meet the colonel's. "It was on the second floor in front of the office of Pearson and Stump. The cleaning woman must have just arrived to clean the next office when she saw me."

"You had been inside the office?" The colonel demanded.

"Yes, sir," Horace admitted.

"And me, sir. I was there too," Max said. "But I came out afterwards, and the woman did not see me," he added.

The colonel went quickly to his desk and pressed an intercom button. "Emergency code red," he barked.

The voice on the other end came in clearly, "Yes, sir."

"We need an immediate tap into the chief of maintenance's line." The colonel turned his head toward Horace and the others. "Silence!"

"Mr. John's line coming through, sir." The colonel raised a paw in warning. Horace barely breathed. A man's voice boomed through the intercom.

"So that's it, Joe. Sorry to bother you this time of night, but it looks like we're going to need an exterminator, and I wanted to give you first crack at it."

"That's some order," a deep voice answered. "With all those gardens, I'll have to bring in quite a crew. I'm busy right now with some old buildings down on Kennedy Street, but I tell you what; let's see first what we're dealing with here. You say the new cleaning lady was hysterical, can't remember much detail? What I'd like you to do is to set up a couple of traps in the office where she thought it came from. Use something like peanut butter. The mice love it. Could be what we have is a field mouse, could be something more. But that building you got there isn't so old, and I can't figure it's much of a problem. You never know though."

"Right, Joe. I wish the woman had been old Dory; she'd have kept her wits about her and swatted the thing. This one was scared out of her mind by the sight of a mouse. I'll set the traps and call you soon as we find something."

"Yeah, otherwise I'll have to come over and do some poking around, put down some poison, see what we need."

"Thanks, Joe. Give my regards to your wife."

"Will do, and I'll be in touch. So long."

The colonel reached over and flipped off the intercom switch. For a moment he covered his eyes with his paw. In a voice drained of energy he said, "The end of a dream. We must do all we can to save ourselves."

Horace felt as if the world was caving in around him. He could not look at Max. As if from far away he heard the colonel say, "Call a meeting of the elders; we've no time to lose."

CHAPTER 10

Mr. Baxter, the elders, and the colonel sat at the council table, their faces solemn. Every eye was upon Horace and Max. Horace's voice shook. "If I hadn't been so blind, so foolish none of this would have happened," he said. "I even persuaded Max to go along with me. This was to have been the final night, the last picture." He hung his head unable to continue.

The colonel looked sternly at Max. "And you, sir, knowingly and willingly aided your friend in this?"

Max's voice was barely a whisper. "I did, sir. I know now I should have persuaded him to forget the paintings."

Standing in the corner, the captain gave a command to Barga, who stood next to him. Barga quickly left the room. Meanwhile the elders talked in low voices to the colonel and Mr. Baxter.

When Barga and one of his men came into the room carrying several large paintings, all talk stopped. "Here's the evidence, sir," Barga said as he and his man dumped Horace's paintings on the table. The colonel picked up one and laid it down again. One of the elders spread the pictures out so that several could be clearly seen.

Mr. Baxter stared at the works, a look of astonishment on his face. "Remarkable," he said, "astounding."

Bright splashes of color seemed to bring the scenes pictured alive, but the colonel barely glanced at them.

"This is what you did night after night? You risked the lives of the entire community for pleasure?" The colonel shook his head. Anger passed over his face like a wave. "Burn them. All of them," he commanded.

Horace swallowed hard. It was what he deserved.

Barga gathered them up in his arms as if they were no more than a heap of trash. On his way out Horace heard him mutter, "Rubbish, that's what they are."

Mr. Baxter cleared his throat. "I fear, you might as well have tried to hold back the garden from blooming. Such a talent as we've seen tonight I have never seen or heard of before among mousedom," Mr. Baxter said.

"Laws made for the safety and good of all this community must not be broken," the colonel thundered, his face stern as he glared at Horace. "Sooner or later this skill Mr. Baxter speaks of would have come to light and found its rightful place here in the community. But you could not wait. The first time you broke the law, you both became guilty of a serious crime, one that has brought us to a terrible crossroads." The colonel no longer looked at Horace or Max as he spoke. "For years we have lived here in peace, secure from hardships that face our kind out in the world every day. We have learned much and advanced beyond the knowledge and skills of other mice. Now we face the loss of everything because of your foolish, thoughtless actions. We will begin evacuating at once." The colonel placed a paw over his heart as if it pained him. Horace saw it and winced.

Every face was stern except for one, Mr. Baxter's. His eyes held a deep look of sadness and concern, and they were directed straight at Horace and Max. "Colonel, gentlemen," Mr. Baxter said. "May I speak? I believe I have a plan." All eyes, including Max and Horace's, turned to stare at Mr. Baxter. "Colonel, you told me once that on the seventh floor of this building there is a lab that uses white mice for testing new cosmetic products."

"Yes," the colonel answered. "Our security check of the building has documented the lab and several cages of white mice, but what has that to do with our present crisis?"

Mr. Baxter continued. "I am, as you know, a white mouse." The silence in the room grew heavy. "And before my escape I was a lab mouse, though that was years ago and miles from here. I am the one they must find in the trap."

His statement met with stunned looks. Then the colonel sputtered, "Nonsense, dear friend. We would not allow it. Besides how would that help?"

"Ah, but you must allow it. You see, I know that the numbers of lab mice change frequently. New ones are bought, some die, and occasionally one of the lab helpers makes a mistake keeping count. I know these things happened when I was a lab mouse. Maintenance must find me in their trap. It will work. Indeed it must, or this entire community is in danger of extermination. Can you move a whole community in two days in the middle of winter?"

One of the elders spoke, his voice low. "If a white lab mouse is found in the trap, the humans will think that it was an escaped mouse the cleaning woman saw and nothing more. We all heard the exterminator say on the phone that our building isn't old. They won't be looking for a large problem. One lab mouse might be the answer." He did not look at Mr. Baxter. No one else spoke.

Mr. Baxter's voice was clear and steady. "I am that mouse. It is settled. I have lived long and well, thankfully, and I am ready." He looked around at them with burning eyes. "All creatures must one day leave this life, and if I go sooner for a greater good, it will be well." He turned to the colonel. "Come, my dear friend. You will grieve, but one day you will join me along with all these," his paw swept the room. "You must believe that I am ready."

The colonel lowered his head and a sob escaped his throat, but with great effort he straightened and looked at his friend. "Joseph, are you sure?"

"Very sure," Mr. Baxter answered.

The colonel did not speak for a moment. He stared long at his friend before speaking. "For the sake of the lives of the young and the old who could not survive a long hard winter march, and the many lives that would otherwise be lost, you will sacrifice your own? I fear that if this is your noble purpose, then I cannot persuade you to do otherwise. It will be as you have said, and we will trust it will be enough." The colonel's voice broke. His glance fell on Horace and Max. A look of anger passed over his face. "Go back to your quarters. I will deal with you later."

Horace felt numb. "No, no. Not Mr. Baxter!" Horace was the one who deserved to die, but he looked down at his gray fur in despair and knew that only a white mouse would do. Mr. Baxter was the only white mouse in the community. Moving like someone in a dream, he followed Max and two guards. Max walked with his head down in a slow heavy way as if he too were part of Horace's terrible dream. Inside the tunnel Max was taken to his own quarters and Horace to his. The door

stood open, the curtain to the bedroom studio pulled back. Where the paintings had been, empty spaces bore traces of the putty he'd use to hang them. His heart felt as if it would break.

For a long time he sat in the old armchair. His mind pictured the great ugly trap and Mr. Baxter stooping over it to touch the bait that would spring the trap and crush his life. He shuddered, but he couldn't even offer himself in Mr. Baxter's place. He was a gray mouse, a good-for-nothing gray mouse who had done a terrible thing. He might as well have been the one to pull the trigger on the trap. It was all his fault. In spite of himself his eyes finally closed. He did not awaken when morning came and others began their day.

In his room Horace woke to the crackling sound of the teapot as it warmed over the sand pit fire as he sat and waited, though he wasn't sure for what. Overground hours had begun when a knock came at his door. This time it wasn't Barga, but a new recruit. "You're to come with me now," the young man said. "Your friend Max has run off like the coward he is, but you'll do." Horace stood too stunned to move. Max was no coward. Something must have happened, but what? Or maybe Max felt it was the only thing he could do. The guard shoved Horace into the hall and back along the tunnel to the gardens.

Long lines of mice stood quietly on every path, all of them looking toward the little knoll on which the colonel, Mr. Baxter, and the elders stood. The guard nudged Horace and together they walked past the silent lines up to the knoll. Horace felt his face flaming. His heart raced like a condemned criminal on his way to justice. Someone in the crowd whispered "courage" and he turned to see. It was Aunt Hanna, her face streaming tears. Horace felt his own eyes fill. What followed took his breath away.

Mr. Baxter stepped forward, placed an arm around Horace's shoulders, and turned him to face the crowds below. "My dear comrades," he began. "You have all come to see me one last time, and I am deeply honored." He paused, then went on. "What I do tonight is my own choice, my high privilege. I have great peace so that I go willingly. You must not grieve for me, but live well the lives you have been given. But I have something to ask of you." The crowds continued to listen in silence.

"This young man has been my friend and yours." A low murmur began below the knoll. Mr. Baxter raised his paw. "Peace, my children. His mistake was not meant to harm anyone. After tonight there will be healing, and life will go on. I ask you to remember that there are two among you who will need healing more than all of you. Do not hold in your hearts anger or bitterness. You must forgive each other. I ask you to forgive." Mr. Baxter hugged Horace to himself, and Horace wept as he had never wept before. When at last Mr. Baxter released him, Horace watched his old friend as he raised a white paw in a last farewell and said. "I am ready, Colonel."

The colonel nodded to his men, and the escort took their positions at the head of the group. The colonel extended his arm to Mr. Baxter. "We will stay with you to the end."

Mr. Baxter nodded. Horace still stood where he was. "Wait," Mr. Baxter said. "I would like Horace with me too."

"Come," the colonel said softly. As Horace followed the little procession, his chest ached and his legs trembled. Behind them a low sobbing had broken out. At the forbidden garden border, the escort stopped to help Mr. Baxter over the ledge. Hardly knowing what he was doing, Horace followed. They had just turned the corner of the landing when a shout rang out behind them.

A single voice called above the rest, "Wait, wait." It was Max and two young mice with him, struggling to carry what looked like a plastic bag with something white in it. The escort guards bristled, their gleaming, sharp-edged weapons held tightly in paws ready for use.

CHAPTER 11

"You," the colonel took a step towards Max. His expression changed from a look of outrage to puzzlement. "What is going on here?" Astonished, Horace stared closely at the clear plastic bag Max and his helpers were carrying. It was a dead mouse, a white one with a metal band around one of its legs.

Breathing heavily, Max explained. "I remembered that I'd seen some dead lab mice in the garbage bins once when I was foraging with one of the teams. It was a slim hope that I'd find one tonight, but there it was, sir."

The colonel bent to look at the plastic bag.

"Sir," Max replied. "We can use the dead lab mouse to take Mr. Baxter's place. Didn't he say that sometimes lab mice escaped and other times the lab workers miscount? Supposing one of the workers put this one in a plastic garbage bag thinking it was dead but on the way down it revived, gnawed its way out of the bag and escaped?"

The captain quickly added, "We could make the bag look as if it had been gnawed and throw it back into the garbage bin, sir."

"Yes, yes," the colonel said. "With that metal tag around his leg, the lab will have to own up that it's one of theirs, or *was* one of theirs. Hurrah," he exclaimed with a loud clap on Max's shoulder. "Well done, lad. Mr. John, chief of maintenance, will assume it's the fault of the lab once he's spotted that tag, and nothing they say will change his mind. Hurry, Captain. You men, take up the body. And report back to me as soon as it's done." Willing hands lifted the plastic bag and its contents and quickly followed the captain to the second floor. The colonel turned to Mr. Baxter. "You're free, Joseph, but we shall never forget what you did. Come, all of you. We have some waiting to do back at headquarters."

The expected call came shortly after curfew had begun. Horace, standing by Max, leaned forward to listen as the colonel quietly tapped into the line, his paw raised for silence.

"Joe?" one of the voices said, "you were right, the trap worked, and we've got our mouse. It's one of the lab mice from that lab on the seventh floor. We got positive ID from the metal tag on its leg. Lab keeps records of all their mice. Records say that one was dead, and one of the workers disposed of it in the usual plastic bag. But this one must have still been alive. Looks like it came to. We found the plastic bag with one end gnawed through. It escaped, and that's how the cleaning lady came to see it running around. Lucky we caught it so quickly. You were right about setting the trap with peanut butter. That's all it was, one escaped lab mouse. The first time anybody's ever seen anything around here in all the years I've been chief."

"That's great, John," the voice on the other end of the line exclaimed. "I'm up to my ears in work, and it sounds to me like you've found the culprit. No sense making a big fuss. One mouse in all this time, and a lab mouse at that, tells me the only mice in that building are the lab mice. Don't think there's much chance of the same thing happening again either. I expect those lab folks will make mighty sure their dead mice are really dead before they dispose of them. You keep in touch, you hear?"

"Right, Joe. Thanks, pal. Give my best to the family."

The colonel flipped off the switch. Relief showed on his face. Mr. Baxter lifted his paws in silent thankfulness. "Praise be! The life of one poor lab mouse has great meaning for us all tonight."

"For awhile I am ordering curfew to begin one hour earlier." The colonel motioned to the captain. "Take what men you need and see that stricter patrols are set on the garden borders. All outdoors activities are canceled until further notice." The captain saluted and left at once.

Mr. Baxter spoke up quietly. "I should like to hold a meeting in the community underground room to give thanks."

"I planned to call everyone together and explain the events of tonight," the colonel said. "It will be a time to answer questions, and as you suggested, Joseph, a time for thanksgiving. However, we have unfinished business with you two." He looked directly at Horace and Max. "There is still the matter of having broken the strictest law of this community. You are to be confined to your quarters until further notice."

"Yes, sir," Horace said almost at the same moment as Max. To Horace it was quite clear that though he and Max might be forgiven for their crime, they would not escape punishment. He deserved it, but poor Max! Two guards escorted him and Max. "House arrest," Horace said in a low voice to Max.

Max nodded. "I will never forgive myself for letting you get carried away. You're a dreamer," he said. "I'm the one who should have seen that no good comes of breaking the law."

Horace couldn't stand the look of woe on Max's face. "You are the one who saved Mr. Baxter's life, and all of us. If you hadn't thought of the garbage bins and the lab mice, I shudder to think of what might have happened."

Max was firm. "You're the dreamer; I'm the practical one. None of this would have happened if I'd done more to stop it right in the beginning."

Horace swallowed hard. "It's my fault, and we both know it."

The guards had come to the turn in the tunnel where Max had to go one way and Horace the other. With no further words, they parted. Sorrow welled up in Horace and threatened to overflow for his friend. At the door the guard saw Horace inside and left. Horace tried the handle from the inside; it was not locked. The colonel had given a command and expected it to be obeyed. This time he would do just that even if it meant being under house arrest for the rest of his days.

Horace was not invited to the town meeting. Afterwards the captain visited him with a formal message. "Having broken the law with most serious consequences, you and Max are to leave the community of Fleur Gardens as an example to all who might in the future be tempted to follow your example. It has been decided that you are to leave in the spring. Meanwhile you are to stay confined. Meals will be brought to you." The captain's voice had been formal, but now he changed it and spoke more gently. "Horace, we've known each other a long time. What you did and why, I might never fully understand, but Mr. Baxter is right. You are forgiven, and things have turned out for good after all, for most of us that is." He blushed then went on. "If there is anything I can do for you, don't hesitate to ask. I will look in on you when duty allows. It may not be a long confinement, but it's not in my hands."

"Thank you," Horace said in a low voice. "I deserve this and more. I appreciate not having to leave in winter. Will you thank the colonel for me?"

The captain nodded and left, closing the door behind him. In the following days Horace saw no one except the young guard who brought food twice a day.

Prison, could it be worse? Horace thought looking around at his bare walls. At least it was warm and he had food enough. Once he picked up a piece of charcoal and began to draw on a bit of old paper. With a sudden cry, he dropped the charcoal. "Never!" he promised himself. "Never again. Not another line." He could at least deny himself that pleasure. He wondered how Max was doing. Poor Max, he must hate being cooped up, away from everything he loves. The thought made Horace feel heavy, tired as if he'd been working hard. Actually he'd done nothing. At first he had tidied the rooms, shined the kitchen, and done every bit of laundry he could find.

After a while he let things go. Dust had begun to settle on shelves and tables undisturbed by Horace. He did keep the fire in the sand pit going in spite of the fact that a January thaw had set in. Warm breezes hinting of spring to come, swept inside the tunnels through the wire mesh gates. He could feel them seeping in under his door. From what he could tell, the thaw seemed to last for days.

Horace was sitting in the old armchair watching the sand clock slowly drip sand. In a few minutes the guard would come with the evening meal. The knock at his door came lightly and Horace went to open it. "Why Aunt Hanna," he exclaimed. "What are you doing here?"

Aunt Hanna's old face beamed. She pointed to a large basket over her arm. "May I come in? I have your dinner, Horace."

Hurriedly Horace cleared a space on the kitchen table, glancing at the soiled dishes lying unwashed in the sink. "I'm sorry," he apologized, "I wasn't expecting anyone, just the guard, that is."

"Oh, Horace, I'm so glad to see you," Aunt Hanna began as she brought a warm root pie from her basket and placed it on the table. "I guess you don't know, but the weather has been far too mild to be healthy in January, and there is so much sickness that poor Mr. Baxter and the nursing staff can't keep up with it. I'm afraid I shall have to do as your company for a few days. What few men of the patrols aren't sick are badly needed elsewhere." She brought out a large flask of what smelled like hot cherry tea, and a loaf of freshly baked bread. "Please, my dear, eat while I sit and chat with you."

Horace was so excited to see a friendly face that he hardly knew what to say. While he ate Aunt Hanna sat nearby. Her white apron was spotless, her gray fur neatly combed. She was the picture of what Horace had always imagined his mother to be, the mother whose face he couldn't remember.

"Max sends you greetings," she said. Horace nearly dropped his mug of tea. Aunt Hanna smiled. "Yes, indeed, he is doing fine, though being confined in small quarters has made him restless." She glanced about her at the clutter. "I think from the looks of things you're feeling it too."

"You can't imagine," Horace said, "how I've missed seeing you and the others." He hung his head as shame warmed his face. "Of course, I have no right to be anywhere but here." He wanted to ask her about Leta, but didn't dare. She was probably seeing a lot of Barga these days.

Aunt Hanna said nothing for a moment. Her eyes were kindly as she leaned forward. "Horace, why don't you tell me about the pictures, what you hoped to do. I'm certain that there was more to all this than a lark just to see forbidden places."

Horace hesitated, but her kindly face drew him on. "It began as an adventure, just a one-time thing, though we never really intended to go beyond the border. We were searching for a special kind of bean vine that grows close to the high north edge of the garden and suddenly found ourselves on the other side examining the vine where it grew across the ledge. I don't know what came over me, but the next thing I knew Max and I were scampering down the hallway. We knew the place was closed for the weekend, and curfew was a good hour away. One of the doors had this metal slot in it, and Max happened to have his climbing gear in his pack. Once inside I saw the pictures, and before I knew it, we found a bit of charcoal, and I was suddenly sketching away on a piece of scrap paper from the trash can. You can imagine the rest."

"Yes, I guess so," Aunt Hanna said softly. "But what did you hope to do with the pictures?"

Horace looked at her strangely. He'd had plenty of time lately to think about that. "I told myself that no mouse had ever painted such things before. I dreamed that when I finished them all I'd show them to the whole community. Ha!" He thumped his paw against the table. His voice trembled. "I told myself breaking the law didn't matter. I was going to show everyone something great. I didn't think about the risks to others, to the whole community." He covered his eyes with his paw. Ashamed to let Aunt Hanna see the tears of anger that filled them. "I wanted fame so badly I couldn't see the danger to anyone else. Max didn't even matter." Unable to stop himself, he choked on a sob. "You know about my lost brother and mother," he said. "Even if one day they return here, Fleur Gardens will be closed to them, thanks to my disgrace."

Aunt Hanna moved to kneel beside him, and her paws went round his shoulders. "Horace, you might have been the son I never had," she said. "You've been through a terrible time, but you have learned something some others never learn. You've learned to see into your own heart and admit the truth to yourself. It's the first step to healing."

Horace dried his eyes and patted her shoulder. "No one could be kinder than you, Aunt Hanna. I would leave now if the colonel hadn't ordered us under house arrest until spring. I have no heart for disobeying rules again."

Aunt Hanna rose and began to pack her basket with the empty dishes. "That is a good place to start your new life, with a healthy respect for rules meant for our good," she said. "There is good in the end to those who learn from their mistakes. I'll be back tomorrow. Rest well." Aunt Hanna smiled and left.

For the first time in many weeks, Horace slept a deep refreshing sleep. He woke early and began to clear up the untidy kitchen. When the knock on his door came, he hurried to it expecting Aunt Hanna, but it was not she.

 **CHAPTER 12**

The young mouse in the doorway looked far too young to be in uniform. "Come in, please," Horace said.

The new recruit stared at Horace, then cleared his throat. "You are to come with me, sir—captain's orders." Horace imagined the worst. So this was it. The colonel had decided not to wait until spring to expel them after all. Thoughts raced through his mind so that he hardly heard his young escort until a sudden word caught his ear.

"We're to stop and pick up your friend Max too. Every available man is needed."

As they hurried towards Max's place, Horace asked sharply, "What do you mean *needed*?"

"Haven't you heard, sir? Sorry, seeing as how you were—begging your pardon—arrested and all that, you haven't heard. The whole community has come down with a new kind of sickness. Knocks you out with raging fever for days and leaves you weak as a baby. That is if you don't die of the coughing first."

Horace's eyes widened. Aunt Hanna had mentioned

sickness. "Do you mean to say the captain has need of me, and of Max?"

"You said it, sir. We don't have the numbers to man half the patrols. Not long ago, rats were spotted at the west gate, and before the guard could stop them, they did a powerful lot of damage. The gate's been repaired, but all the same the captain is mighty nervous. Here we are, sir." Max looked startled when he saw Horace. Quickly Horace filled him in, and Max hurriedly joined them.

At headquarters the colonel was nowhere in sight. The captain received them with a stern look. "I know this is a bit irregular to order you two into this, but frankly I'm desperate. I'm down to three men for main grounds patrol, and you are two of them."

Horace looked at Max in surprise. "It's that bad?" he asked.

"Yes, and according to Mr. Baxter, this siege of sickness doesn't seem to be loosening its grip yet. I need you both. Will you help?"

Max stood straight. "If you'll have me, I'd like nothing better, sir."

Horace searched the captain's face. "Are you sure you can trust someone like me?"

The captain said nothing for a moment. "I have no question of your loyalty or your ability. Can you trust yourself? It's up to you."

Horace nodded. "All right then. Where do you want us?"

"You will need these," the captain said, tossing each of them a shoulder sash, the insignia of the patrol, "and these," he added, handing them weapons. As he did, he called out, "Ah, Barga, you're just in time. These are your men. They will be your responsibility, and you are to treat them as your patrol with every right and privilege of a patrol guard. I expect you all to work together as a team."

Horace and Max had both swung around to face Barga, who stood gaping at them. "Yes, sir, Captain," Barga said with a sharp salute. To Max and Horace his command was short, "You two wait outside." Horace could not hear what was said behind the closed door, but when Barga came out his face was red, and the look he gave them was like a dark thundercloud. "I may have to follow orders," he muttered "but I don't have to like them. We have grounds duty, and there's no time to spare." Marching swiftly, he led the way to the main gate, where a single guard opened the gate to let them through.

Outside, the darkness of the night and the mildness of the air struck Horace at once. It took him several seconds before his eyes adjusted. A low wind howled around the building. On a clear night the stars would have shone brilliantly, but tonight they were hidden by clouds.

Now that they were outside on duty, Barga's tone sounded more anxious than angry. "We ought to have half a dozen guards patrolling. At least the weather is on our side. The cloud cover is good. Max, you take the north side of the building and then head west. Horace, you take the south side then head west to meet Max. I'll check the east bridge area where the line of trees begins then meet up with you two. Keep your eyes open for anything that moves. Stay close to the building and report back to me at once if there is anything suspicious. The idea is to stay alive, report trouble, and warn the rest of the community. We're not out here to play heroes. Understood?"

Horace heard himself say, "Yes, sir." Max saluted smartly and took off on his route. The building was shaped like a square to the north and a triangle to the south. Once Horace had turned to begin his route along the wall heading south, he could no longer see Barga.

Horace lowered his head as a gust of warm wind hit him full force. How was he supposed to see anything when he could barely keep to the path? He stopped once to peer into the vast grounds across the roadway that ran by this side of the building but saw nothing. If it had been humans surprising the community to worry about, even on a night like this, one could spot a car coming or else hear the motor. He heard nothing but the wind blowing against the building. He never saw what hit him.

Horace woke with a groan. His head hurt too much to move it. As his eyes adjusted to the darkness, he realized he was no longer outside. He was flat on his back in some sort of storage room. Not only that, but his paws were tied with wire! The dimmest of light came from a small crack near the bottom of the nearby wall. Painfully he managed to roll onto his side. To his horror someone else lay only inches away. "Barga, is that you?"

Barga turned to face him. A bloody gash over his right eye and blood on his chest made Horace gasp. "It's me," Barga said mournfully. "I never heard them coming until they were on top of me. Two rats attacked. They were likely the same ones that captured you. You all right?" Barga pushed with his feet until he was leaning against the dirt wall. "Smart of them to use wire or we'd be out of here by now," he said.

Horace tried to move his paws but the bindings were tight. "Right. And it doesn't look like it's worn thin anywhere either," he said. "How long have we been here, and where exactly are we?" Horace asked.

"As near as I can tell, you've been out for an hour. Glad to see you haven't left us for good. From the smallness of the room I'd say it's an old abandoned storage room, except that we're in here. And that puzzles me." Barga stopped and seemed lost in thought. When he spoke, he said, "I've never known rats to take prisoners.

They generally kill. This is most unusual." He coughed, then coughed again.

Horace's head ached. "You don't suppose they plan to torture us or . . ." he couldn't finish.

"Or what?" demanded Barga.

"Nothing. It doesn't make sense. I just had the strangest thought that they might be saving us for something else. They've been watching us for some time now. I'm certain I caught one peering through the window glass Christmas night. When I took a second look, it was gone. Maybe they hope to find out something from us." A shudder ran through him. What did they want?

Barga stared at him. "That's crazy. They're wild. What could they possibly want to know? Except maybe what we have worth stealing."

Horace thought to himself, *And wild mice don't tap into telephone lines or use intercoms, but the mice of Fleur Gardens do.* Aloud he said, "There's no telling what purpose they have in mind. Anyway, does it really matter? We're here, and what I want to know is how do we get out of here."

Barga cleared his throat. "I'm counting on Max. They might not have seen him since he was on the north side of the building. At least he can warn the others."

"What if he didn't see what happened?" Horace had little hope that Max had seen. If he had, he surely would have come barreling in to help.

"He has to know something happened. All he has to do is report back, and the captain will know. If Max is even alive," Barga said. Once more a deep cough racked Barga and left him breathing hard.

Horace looked more closely at Barga. "You're not getting sick too?" he said.

When Barga tried to laugh it sounded more like a raspy chuckle. "What if I am? Do you think the rats will care?"

"I didn't know about the sickness until tonight when the captain sent for us to do guard duty," Horace said. "I hear it has spread throughout the whole community, and it doesn't look like it will let up soon."

"I don't know about the last part, but it's spread all right. If the rats were to launch a large attack any time in the next few days, they'd find little to stop them. We've a single guard on the gates as you saw. The only patrol left was ours."

"You can't mean just the three of us," Horace said horrified. "What about the colonel, the rest of the troops?"

"Most of them sick, others too weak for duty, including the colonel. Fevers, coughs, weak as babies, and nothing seems to work once it hits. Mr. Baxter says it will just have to run its course. The captain's been using youngsters too small to wear the uniforms to do curfew patrols and tunnel patrols. Every available mouse not down with the sickness is needed by the nurses just to keep up with tending sick families."

"I didn't know," Horace said. The sudden rattling of a metal gate startled him.

A deep growling voice sneered, "Neither did we, but thanks to you two we know now. Hee, hee. You want to know why we took you prisoner, eh? Think you're the only ones who know anything, do you? You with your fancy doings, all nice and cozy holed up inside that building. It won't be for long." A terrible laugh followed and footsteps scurried away till their sound died out.

Neither Horace nor Barga could speak their horror at first. Tears of frustration rolled down Horace's face. "They've been spying on us all along," he said.

Finally Barga, struggling between coughing and catching his breath, said in a voice strangely changed to a high squeak, "The devils! They were listening while I told them just what they needed. Now that they know we can't put up much of a fight. They'll attack for certain, and it's my fault. I'm the one to blame," he cried.

"Barga, listen, it's not your fault. I asked if you were getting sick; I started the whole thing. There's no sense blaming; we've got to do something." Desperately Horace strained at his bonds ignoring the pain that nearly blinded him. They were too tight, too expertly twisted for him to reach with his teeth; and even if he could, they were wire, and he wasn't sure he could sever them.

Barga murmured, "It's hopeless, hopeless." His fits of coughing grew more and more frequent. Horace stopped struggling. He lay shivering in the damp cold of their prison. "What can we do?" Barga didn't answer and Horace could think of nothing bound up like they were. If Max was alive, he would surely alert the captain and send a rescue patrol. Only there were no patrols to send, none to spare.

He had no idea what made him think of Aunt Hanna, but her words came to him, *You've learned to see into your own heart and admit the truth to yourself. It's the first step to healing.* The truth was that sooner or later the rats would have figured out how weak the mice patrols were. They'd been planning to take over Fleur Gardens all along! What he needed to do now was think of a way to get out of here. He closed his eyes. When he opened them and turned to look at Barga, he cried out. "Barga what's the matter?" Barga's body shook with tremors. *The fever must be on him*, Horace thought.

Suddenly Barga cried out, "I'm burning." Soon after that he was freezing! Inching his way to Barga's side Horace placed himself as close as he could, hoping to warm him. He closed his eyes once more to think as Barga huddled next to him.

In a small alcove out of the wind, Max had waited for Horace to meet up with him. When no one came, he began to worry that too much time had passed. Carefully he circled the building looking, for Horace and Barga. Close to the path on the south side, he found a bit of torn cloth—part of a patrol insignia sash! Horace had been wearing one. Further search showed what he had missed before—faint signs of something being dragged. There was no sign of Barga. Max followed the marks, losing them, then finding them a little further on toward the south bridge. Close to the bridge they disappeared among the clumps of old winter weeds lining the stream banks. *Rats!* Max thought. Horace must have been attacked by rats and dragged off to their tunnels. That meant either Barga had gone after them or he too had been taken captive. Icy fear filled Max. He had to do something, but what? If he went back, who was there to help beside the captain? And he was needed at headquarters. There was no help.

He looked anxiously around him, wondering if he too was being spied upon by some rat patrol. Seeing nothing, he crept closer to the bridge to take cover and think what to do next. The ice was gone from the stream below him forcing him to walk gingerly along the sloping bank. Under the bridge he sat against the bank and wondered. Suddenly as if a voice had spoken, he remembered the old rat tunnel! Horace had found it the day they'd taken the widow Jem's children sledding. Jumping to his feet he began to search. Under one of the wooden trestles he found the dark hole just wide enough for rats. It looked as if it hadn't been used lately, and there were no prints in the damp earth where the snow had melted. Without thinking he entered.

CHAPTER 13

The wind behind him died to a moaning sound as Max went further into the tunnel. He could hear his heart beating loudly. The tunnel was old, and some of its earth walls were cracked and badly in need of repair. He was surprised that it seemed to angle slightly downward, which would make it dangerous if ever the waters under the bridge rose too high and flooded. *That might have been the reason the rats abandoned it*, he thought. It probably led nowhere now but to some old unused nesting tunnels. Still something urged him on. Suddenly the tunnel ended, and Max was standing in front of a solid stone wall.

He could hear nothing from the other side of the wall. "This must have been built when the rats cut off the old tunnel," he whispered to himself. "Why cut off the old tunnel unless they planned to keep any water from getting

through it to nests and tunnels on the other side of the wall? They've built another main tunnel entry somewhere else," he told himself. He started back the way he had come. There was a smaller tunnel to the left, but he had ignored it wanting to reach the end of the big tunnel first. He would examine that one too.

Like the main tunnel, there were no signs that the smaller one had been used for some time. He found himself turning several times, away from the old tunnel to what seemed to be even lower ground. A feeling of urgency came over him so strongly that he could not have turned back. "Is this where I am supposed to be going?" He heard no answer, but the urgent feeling that he must go on kept him moving, and he pressed forward. Within a few feet the tunnel ended abruptly. There was simply nothing ahead of him but dirt. He leaned wearily against the packed earth. It was all a mistake. There was little more he could do on his own. He would have to go back and report his failure to the captain, who by now knew that three of his men were missing. He had turned to go when he thought he heard something. With his ear against the dirt wall he listened. Voices! They seemed to be coming from a small break near the bottom of the wall where one of the cracks had widened.

"Come on, Barga. You must sit up."

Heavy coughing followed and then, "I'll try, Horace. I can't breathe like this."

Max nearly jumped for joy. He might have begun to pound on the wall in front of him and shout that he was coming, but something stopped him. *Get a grip on yourself*, he scolded. *Someone else might be in there too.* He thought for a moment and then began to scrape away as quietly as he could at the bottom of the wall in front of him. The dirt, though once packed hard, had loosened so that it came away more easily than he had feared.

Carefully he dug using the end of his weapon until he had what he wanted: a hole large enough to glimpse inside.

As soon as his eyes had adjusted, he saw what appeared to be a room and two figures he knew must be Horace and Barga. They sat against the wall to the right of him.

"Psst. Psst. Over here. At the bottom of the wall. Can you see the hole?" Max whispered.

Horace looked wildly towards him, "Is that you, Max? I can't see you. Thanks be, you've come."

"It looks like you two are alone in there," Max said in a whisper.

"The guards seem to have left us. I think we're in some kind of jail. Can you get us out?" Horace asked keeping his voice low.

"I'm going to dig my way through, but keep a sharp eye and let me know if you hear anyone coming," Max ordered. Sweat poured from him as he dug. He knew he ought to be shoring up the old wall with beams, but there was nothing to use and no time to go back. He could only trust there wouldn't be a cave-in while he worked. The hole he made was small, but big enough for a mouse. It would have to do. Max wriggled through and hurried to Horace and Barga.

As he worked at the wires binding Horace, he explained how he'd found them. "There, you're free," Max said, turning to begin working on Barga. All this time Barga had barely spoken, though the coughing continued every little while.

Horace rubbed the feeling back into his limbs, and limping but determined, went to help Barga. "Why you're burning up with fever," he whispered as he touched Barga's hot legs.

"Leave me and go while you can," Barga murmured. "You have to save the others," he said weakly.

"We've no time to explain now," Horace said to Max. "Every second counts. The rats know about the sickness in the community, and we must warn the captain." He turned back to Barga, who stooped over in anguish as the blood rushed to the places that had been so tightly bound. "You're coming with us, if we have to drag you," Horace whispered fiercely.

For part of the way they did drag Barga, who could barely walk in spite of their help, but neither Max nor Horace stopped to shift Barga's heavy weight or rest. At the old tunnel's end the fresh night air held the welcome smell of freedom. They still had to reach the building and the east gate, only now with their goal in sight, Horace felt a new strength. Even Barga seemed to straighten a little though he still clung to Horace and Max's shoulders.

They were in sight of the gate when the captain and two others came running toward them. Willing hands relieved Horace and Max of their burden. As the gate closed behind them, Horace breathed heavily and could barely find voice enough to say, "Thanks to you, Max, we're safe. But only for the moment, I fear." Turning to the captain he said, "Sir, my report is urgent. The rats are aware of our weakened defenses and are planning an attack to take the community."

The captain's face paled. "I feared something like this. Hurry," he commanded. Two female mice were already escorting Barga to sickbay. Horace and Max followed the captain and his young guards.

"A handful of the men are up and about, able to fight, but we are hopelessly outnumbered by any normal, healthy rat pack. Without a patrol to keep them back, they'll no doubt use battering rams to breach the gates. Our gates will not withstand much of that." The captain covered his eyes but only for a moment. Motioning to one of the new recruits, he gave orders for six of the guards to be called, half of them to be posted at the east gate, the others at the west gate. "We must do all we can," he said.

Horace suddenly remembered that the last time he'd seen food or drink was back in his room. His stomach rumbled loudly. Max looked at him knowingly. The captain seemed lost in thought, but he glanced over to Horace and pointed to a tea service on the corner of his desk. Someone had piled sandwiches on a platter next to it. "Help yourself."

"Thank you, sir," Horace said. The captain's attention seemed lost again, and he didn't respond. Horace handed Max the platter and took a seed sandwich himself. Actually, he was thirsty. As he poured the tea, he noticed the stains on what was left of his sash. The floor of the rat prison had been damp and muddy. "Mud," he said rubbing at it with one paw.

"Not surprised," Max said. "The floor of that place was lower even then the other old tunnel the rats abandoned. They probably had flooding in spring and decided to build a new entry tunnel on high ground. The old tunnel ended at a stone wall. From the looks of the wall they'd done a good job to keep out any water. I think their nesting tunnels are behind that stone wall."

"Then we must have been in one of the old storage rooms from when the first tunnel was still in use. No wonder they kept it for a jail. It was far too wet for anything else but prisoners," Horace said. "Too bad we couldn't dig a small opening like the one you made, Max, and flood their whole place out."

The captain had risen to join them. "Is it possible? Could our men undermine the stone wall enough for water to seep under it?"

"I suppose," Max said. "But it's a big risk. Anyone on the other side might discover it before you were even through the wall. And where would the water come from?

We haven't had enough snow this winter for a flood even with the melted snow that's in the stream now."

"Yes, Max, but you forget that stream is spring fed from underground on the east side of the bridge," Horace said. "That's why I noticed the seepage that made the mud in the jail. There must be stairs leading up from the jail to the main tunnels above, and probably a good stout flood gate at the top."

The captain's voice was excited. "The water from the underground spring runs beneath into the stream and, with nothing to block it, keeps running on its way north of the bridge. How much work would it be for a crew to dam the north side and divert the water into the old tunnel? We'd need another crew to make the opening under the stone wall."

Stunned at the thought, Horace stared at the captain. "You mean flood out the rat's nesting tunnels?" Once the waters began rising, there would be no way to stop it! "By now the rats will know we're gone, and they may be planning an attack any time," Horace pointed out. "On the other hand, they may just have intended to leave us there to die of starvation and don't even know we're gone."

"You're right. Rats are strange creatures set in their ways, and they are not known for their mercy to cap-tives," the captain said. "It's possible that it never oc-curred to them that mice might attack using their old tunnel. Besides, thanks to you, they think we're all down sick, and whoever isn't sick will be guarding our gates. They're probably laughing at us right now as they plan. If we work quickly and are successful, we could take them by surprise!"

Horace stepped forward. "I volunteer, Captain, for digging duty. Max and I have worked on tunnel repairs long enough to know how to undo one. No matter how far down those stones go, with some good pipe we'll get through that wall. The force of rushing waters will do the rest."

Several mice recovered from illness had come into the office to stand quietly, listening to the conversation. One by one, they volunteered to build the dam. Horace recognized two of them from his former tunnel crew.

"I can't guarantee you much help should anything go wrong. None to be exact," the captain said looking glum. "And I don't need to point out the dangers to any of you. You're a brave crew. I pray you will succeed. "

Max saluted. "With your permission, sir, I know where the tools we'll need are stored."

"Take all you need, and know that our thoughts go with you too."

The timing would have to be exact. Max and Horace must be finished before the dam crew could begin its work, or they would drown. The crews, now grown larger by several new recruits, knew exactly what to do. They had long ago learned well the ways of the

beavers whose dams were the best in the wild. Working under cover of the night with great twisted vine ropes, they slid giant limbs fallen from oaks and other hardwoods across the thin layers of snow still lying in the deep woods. From there the logs were dragged on large sleds of greased cloth to the bank of the stream and slid quietly in place. Others, risking their lives on the growing heap, wove sticks and branches into the wall of wood. No one spoke. The work went on almost noiselessly. Two of the crew filled in the opening of the smaller tunnel leading to the place where Horace and Barga had been held. It would be enough to divert the water into the main tunnel.

Inside the tunnel Max was well below the wall of stone. Horace laid his paw on Max's shoulder signaling him to wait. "Let me take a look before we fit the pipe in place," he whispered. Around their waists each wore a safety line meant to guide them back in case of an emergency.

Max stood back revealing the large hole under the stone wall. "Be careful, mate."

Horace nodded and crawled into the hole. It angled upward, and loose dirt came sifting down on him at every move. He shook the dirt from his head and pushed himself upward. As his eyes adjusted, he could see they had indeed come out into a main tunnel. Not far beyond him was the first nesting tunnel, and it was open! The rats had no doors such as the mice of Fleur Gardens did. Quickly Horace eased himself backwards. Max had already lugged the great pipe to the hole. "You've done it, Max. The nests are right above us," he whispered.

Max grinned. Together they inched the large, widemouthed pipe in place. It angled just right to fit Max's diggings. Max crawled through it once to make sure nothing blocked the opening and slid back out with a satisfied look on his face. Horace was about to congratulate him when he felt something cold slosh around his feet. Water!

Max's face turned pale as his feet too felt the rising water. Running for their lives, the two raced to the tunnel's mouth feeling the cords around their middle grow tight as crewmen above the bridge's wooden trestle pulled. They reached the outside of the tunnel just as the icy waters closed over Horace's head. Hanging on with all his strength Horace felt himself floating strangely, and then a hard jerk lifted him clear of the water. In seconds he felt the grip of many strong paws. Others lifted a dazed Max to safety. Horace's legs felt weak, his head spun, but he pulled himself to his feet to watch the water rising below. "It's working," he whispered in amazement.

Max looked at Horace and grinned, then back at the water. His voice too was full of wonder. "Look at that, mate, the dam is really holding."

"Knew it would," one of the crew said. "Let's get out of here before the whole rat pack comes running."

CHAPTER 14

"Mission accomplished, sir," Horace said saluting from under the blanket that covered his dripping fur. The rest of the crew had slipped into the office behind him and Max. The captain stood up from behind his desk as they entered. He looked as if he hadn't slept for days. Papers and charts covered the desk. A tray of sandwiches and pots of tea sat on one end of it.

A pleased expression softened the lines on the captain's face as he listened carefully to the report. "All we can do now is trust that we've given the rats something else to think about while our men recover their strength," he said. "You have all done brave work tonight. Better get some sleep. Horace, you and Max will have to bed down here for the night. We've taken over every available spot in the east tunnel."

Sleeping mats lay strewn in a corner, and Horace nodded as he headed towards them. He suddenly felt too weary for words. The next thing he knew someone was shaking him by the shoulder. "Time to wake up, mate." It was Max bending over him. "The colonel is here," he whispered.

Horace stood up at once, brushing down rumpled fur and feeling a sinking in his stomach. The old feeling of shame came back to settle over him as he looked at the colonel.

The colonel sat down at his desk and picked up the report in front of him. Silently he read the report, then laying it aside, motioned to Horace and Max. "Sit down, sit down," he said. "First let me congratulate you both on your quick thinking and courage. We have you and your brave crew to thank that this community is not presently overwhelmed by our late neighbors the rats."

Horace was puzzled. "*Late* neighbors?"

"Yes," the colonel explained. "Our patrol scouts reported them leaving the park in a mass just before dawn. They have obviously moved on to one of their former quarters, thanks to you. The warm weather, too, has been on our side. The stream is in full flood. I doubt they will ever build so close to one again." He paused. "Now for some unfinished business I would like to discuss."

Horace wondered what the colonel meant. Did the sudden change in the weather mean they were to begin their exile now? "I suppose if the rats can leave now there is no reason for Max and me not to go." He nodded to show that he understood they were to be expelled from the community.

"Yes, sir," Max said quietly.

"A month ago I would have agreed," the colonel said, "but you two have risked your lives to save this community. Your noble deeds have canceled any remaining sentence for your former mistakes. You may stay and be welcome in this community on your solemn word that you will never again set foot beyond the garden borders unless authorized by me or my replacement to do so. What do you say?"

Horace looked at Max but could not read his face. "Sir, I appreciate your offer with all my heart. As to breaking the laws of this community, I have no problem giving my word that I will obey them with all my heart." Horace paused and felt his face grow warm. "But I am not sure I deserve to stay here, sir," he said. Silence followed his statement.

The colonel cleared his throat. "You understand that you are both truly welcome to stay? It would grieve me personally to see you go." His voice was sincere.

Max spoke then. "I thank you for your kindness, sir, but what Horace said goes for me too."

The colonel looked deep into Horace's eyes and then into Max's as if he could read their very thoughts somehow. "Do not forget Mr. Baxter's words about going on with life, living well, forgiving others, all said when he thought his own death was at hand. I will not speak of it again, but you have given your word to obey the laws of this community, and you have paid your debt at the risk of your own lives." The colonel reached out to rest a large paw on Horace's right shoulder and Max's left. "You have the thanks of this whole community for what you have done to save it. From now on, live well." Cheers broke out from the captain and the men of the patrols standing near him.

"Thank you, sir," Horace's voice was husky.

Beside him Max grinned broadly. "Aye, and it's glad we are to be here, Colonel," he said. "The world out there is a big challenge, if you know what I mean."

The captain smiled. "There was a time when I was your age and ready to take on the world. But I had my calling to stay here and help make Fleur Gardens a safe and thriving place. We need your kind here."

Horace smiled. "Thank you, sir."

Max saluted. "Thank you, sir."

The colonel waved them off with one paw as he picked up a paper from the pile of work waiting on his desk. "You may report back to your work crews. Repairs are badly needed on the east gate, and there's work to be done in the tunnels." Before Horace and Max could reach the door the colonel's voice halted them. "By the way, Horace, before you go I have one more question."

Feeling like a load had been lifted from his shoulders Horace was ready for anything. "What is that, sir?"

"Your paintings were actually quite impressive. I suppose you might not mind using your talents to do a scene or two around here? Perhaps something for the office here, and one or two for the meeting hall?"

Ideas ran through Horace till he thought he would burst with excitement. "I'd be honored, I mean glad, sir, to be of use." He could barely keep from running from the office and nearly knocked into a stack of boxes in his path. Already what scenes to paint and the materials he could use occupied his thoughts. When the door shut behind them, Horace threw his arms around Max's shoulders and practically lifted him from the floor. "Did you hear that, Max? I can paint, and this time he's just about promised to display them." It was a dream come true.

Max thumped Horace's back heartily and then looked him in the eye. "Give you a bit of charcoal or a paint brush, and there's no telling what will come of it." Max couldn't hold back a glad shout. It brought an abrupt look of surprise to his face. "Didn't know I had that in me," he said. "Come on, mate. We've got work to do."

"And planning, Max," Horace said in a more serious voice. "Max, have I told you that, whatever comes of all this, there is no one I'd rather have with me than you, my friend? The colonel is right," he added, "if the community is going to thrive, they'll need mice like you."

Max nodded. "I think he said mice like us. All the same, mate, two heads are better than one, even if yours is going to float off one of these days with all those daydreams." Max thumped a paw on Horace's shoulder and laughed loudly.

"Wait a minute," Horace said, "whose head is so full of practical schemes like how to get hold of one of Miss Bea's berry cakes? Not to mention anything like warm bread or seed and apple cookies. Do I need to go on?" For the rest of the way, the two tired friends were merry as they walked to the east tunnel.

Word of the flood and the exodus of the rats had spread quickly, and as Horace and Max entered the tunnel, their old work crew came to surround the two. "Good to have you back," one said, and others echoed him. For the first time in weeks Horace didn't feel shame welling up inside him as he faced old friends. It was gone! No one asked about the colonel, and neither Horace nor Max said anything about the colonel's words to them. For now it was just good to be back with the crew and at work again.

It had been a perfect morning until the noon lunch arrived. Leta was one of the servers. Her gray fur shone, and a dainty ribbon graced her neck. The basket on her arm brimmed with hot root pasties smelling of lemon grass. She stopped in front of Horace and held out her basket. "It's good to see you, Horace. We've all heard about what you and Max did. You're heroes! I made these myself. Please have some."

Horace's face grew warm as he struggled for the right words. "There were a lot of us involved in all that. But thanks, these smell wonderful." He took a hot pasty. He could think of nothing else to say and looked down at the pasty in his paw. It was really hot, and he flipped it between his paws.

"Oh dear," Leta said, "I should have given you a napkin to hold it. I know they're quite warm." She handed him a paper napkin.

"Thanks," Horace said as he took it. He knew he ought to say something more, but couldn't. Leta smiled and went on to offer lunch to others.

Max with two pasties in a napkin plopped down beside Horace. "Saw you talking to Leta. Does she know the colonel's no longer planning to put us out?"

"Didn't mention it," Horace said. Leta would have been the one Horace most regretted to leave behind had the colonel banished them. "Reckon she and Barga will make a good pair once he's back on his feet," he said. "Leta and her aunt have had enough trouble in their lives. They lost everything once. At least here they can live in peace."

Max finished a bite of pasty. "You're right, mate. With the rats quiet for a while there ought to be little to keep this community from flourishing. I hate to think what might have happened after that cleaning lady spotted us. Best not to look back, but I do think the colonel has tightened up the controls a good bit. Thankfully, everything turned out for good."

"Yes," Horace agreed. He turned to watch the graceful form of Leta as she left, her basket empty, her paw raised in a quick goodbye. Horace sighed and looked at the half-eaten pasty in his paw. She had made it. He nibbled what was left till all that remained was a small circle. Folding the napkin around it he put it into his pack. The brown crusted morsel, when dipped into gold paint and dried, would become one of his keepsakes. With another sigh he joined the others already at work on the gate.

CHAPTER 15

The night air in the indoor gardens carried mingled scents of crocuses and sweet mint to Horace as he painted. He had placed his easel near the north border to paint the gardens below. The picture in front of him looked so real he could almost believe the painted flowers were sending out their sweetness. Now and then someone came to watch, but for the moment he was alone. He stopped to stretch his paws and saw Max heading toward the cherry tea stand below. On his arm a well-rounded Miss Bea chatted away. He couldn't hear them from this distance, but Max, who had spotted him, waved. And Horace waved back. A moment later he saw Leta. She wasn't alone.

Fully recovered, though a bit thinner from his illness, Barga was guiding Leta along the path. The two seemed to be talking earnestly. Horace watched them for a moment, then turned away, picked up his paintbrush and began painting furiously.

"Ahem." The voice behind him made Horace turn quickly. Mr. Baxter stood with his paws clasped, his cheerful face beaming. "Horace, the garden looks so real on your canvas I can almost smell the flowers. You have a fine talent, son. I wonder, have you thought of teaching some of the young ones around here, perhaps even starting a small class?"

Horace laid his brush on the easel's ledge. As he did he glanced below just as Barga handed a cup of cherry tea to Leta. Horace swallowed hard and looked at Mr. Baxter. "No, no, I expect with spring coming, I'll be leaving here to try my way in the world out there. So I can't stay and teach, I'm afraid." He felt his face grow warm. He had just this moment decided he would leave Fleur Gardens as soon as possible.

Mr. Baxter touched Horace's shoulder lightly. "Since the day I gave you your mother's gift, I've expected this. You may not find what you hope for, but your search may help piece together some of what happened after the great fire. I'm proud of you, Horace."

A deep blush of shame filled Horace. He hadn't thought of looking for his brother even once since his capture by the rats. But it was time he did! He turned to say something to Mr. Baxter, but before he could say a word, Mr. Baxter cleared his throat and pointed to the gardens below.

"Well now, isn't that Barga below? Quite recovered, I see, and Miss Leta is with him. I say, she is lovely." He smiled at Horace. "When you go, I will miss our talks. You were one of my star pupils, you know. I should have liked to see you in my place one day passing on the traditions. I am not getting any younger, Horace." Mr. Baxter's old face was wrinkled with years and his gray whiskers tinged with white. "It may be that you will come back to us," he added.

Horace shut his eyes for a second and opened them. "I can't say when I'd likely get back. But I would do anything for you, sir, that I could." He loved this old mouse, but now that he'd made up his mind to leave Fleur Gardens there was no turning back. The ivory carving still around his neck suddenly seemed to make him anxious to go. Somewhere out there a brother he truly longed to know might be wearing the other half.

Mr. Baxter's eyes searched Horace's face. "Will Max go with you?" he asked.

"Well, ah, I don't know. I haven't spoken to him yet," Horace replied stumbling for words.

"So this decision of yours to leave come spring is a recent one, I take it?" Mr. Baxter asked.

"Yes, sort of, that is. There's not much to keep me," Horace said, and quickly regretted his words. "I mean, sir, that I really do want to look for my brother." As he spoke the words, all the longing for a family he'd never known welled up in his heart, and Horace knew that he wanted to search for them more than ever.

Mr. Baxter smiled. "Good, son. But may I ask you one favor before you go? The colonel has requested that you do a portrait for the meeting hall, something for the historical record. Ah, actually my portrait, though I hardly think of myself as a historical figure." Mr. Baxter laughed. "The colonel was quite taken with the portrait you did of him."

"I'd be honored," Horace answered. A rush of feeling went through him. Why hadn't he thought of it before? A portrait of Mr. Baxter was the very thing the community needed, and he could do it. "I'll be finished here tonight. I could begin tomorrow if you like."

Mr. Baxter nodded. "How about late morning, say ll:00 by the sand clock at my place, if that is good for you."

"I'll be there," Horace said picking up his brush to add a last detail. As Mr. Baxter left, Horace watched the old mouse walking slowly, stopping to greet friends. He would miss him terribly. By the time curfew warning sounded, he'd finished the painting. With the easel under his arm he hurried toward his tunnel.

A breathless Max caught up with him in the tunnel. "Wait up, mate. What's this I hear about you leaving? I bumped into Mr. Baxter, and he asked if I'd be going along." Max stood still and waited for an answer.

"Sorry, Max. I would have told you myself. I just decided tonight. You were busy with Miss Bea or I'd have let you know. I have to try to find my brother, Max. And as soon I wrap up things here, I want to begin." Horace shifted the easel under his arm. "I've promised to do a portrait of Mr. Baxter first. We start tomorrow. As soon as it's done, I'll be ready." Horace would have given anything to have Max along, but he'd seen the look on Max's face whenever Miss Bea came around.

"Would you believe it, mate, that I was just telling Miss Bea I'd most likely be heading out come spring? Made up my mind to do some searching, a bit of exploring. I was sure hoping you'd come along," Max said and grinned. "Now that you're planning on going, we might as well travel together."

Words stuck in Horace's throat, and he swallowed hard. "You don't fool me for a minute," he said. "But if a fellow like you can really walk away from Miss Bea's kitchen knowing it will be lean pickings out there, and maybe worse, then you are more addle-headed than I thought. I guess that makes two of us, old buddy."

Max smiled broadly. "Alright then, it's settled; we'll search together, and the sooner the better, I say."

On the following morning Horace began his final painting. Mr. Baxter sat in a large armchair looking dignified in his best Sunday outfit. Horace sketched carefully. By noon Mr. Baxter called for a lunch break. At the same moment a soft knock on the door sounded, and a light voice called, "May I come in?"

"Ah, Leta," Mr. Baxter cried. "Come in, child, come in." He turned to Horace as Leta entered carrying a large basket. "I arranged for Leta to bring our lunch. Nothing like a fine lunch to keep one fit for work," he said. He smiled and invited Leta to sit with them.

Her eyes sparkled as she thanked him. "I'm expected at Miss Bea's in a few minutes, or I'd love to join you."

"Tomorrow then," Mr. Baxter said. "Since I've hired your services, you really must stay and have lunch with us."

"I'd like that, and tomorrow would be fine," Leta said.

"Consider it done," Mr. Baxter insisted.

Horace had been standing speechless all the while. When the door shut behind her, he realized he was still holding a piece of charcoal.

"So how long do you think my picture will take?" Mr. Baxter asked. "Not that I'm in a hurry, just wondering how many lunches we might arrange for Leta to bring."

"Oh," Horace said thinking quickly. "I'd like to be sure of the colors once I start painting. Could be a week."

"Hmph," Mr. Baxter said. "Sit down and eat."

On the following day Leta stayed to eat with them. First she inspected the picture. "I think it's going to be great," she said. "Even the sketch truly is you, Mr. Baxter."

"Too bad, don't you think," Mr. Baxter said, "that our friend here won't stay around a bit longer. I fear we will be losing him and Max shortly."

Leta looked up at Horace with surprise in her dark eyes. "You are going, then? I thought, or at least I heard, that the colonel had welcomed you to stay after all you and Max did to save the community."

Horace put the seed cake he was holding down next to the berry jam. "I've decided to go," he said quietly. He said nothing of his reasons.

"Oh, I see." Leta's voice was low. She busied herself with spreading jam on a bit of apple bread. "Well then, so long as you're going, have you a place in mind? I'd be glad to tell you what I know of places on the outside that I've heard about."

Horace cleared his throat. He had no plans yet. "I thought we might head west or southwest maybe, Max and I."

"There are places like old warehouses in the city," Leta continued, "but most of them are already occupied, and strangers aren't always welcome." For the rest of the lunch they talked about the possibilities—railroad stations, farms, theaters. The list grew longer. As they talked, Horace wondered if he was making a mistake. How could he ever find his brother? Would there ever be another place like Fleur Gardens community?

"Oh," Leta said, "I forgot to mention a place Barga told me about. He heard there was an old abandoned factory on the outskirts of the city." At the mention of Barga's name, Horace forgot everything else. The sooner he left the better.

On the fourth day when Leta came with the lunch, Mr. Baxter suddenly remembered another luncheon date.

"Leta, be a dear and stay here with Horace. You two eat up that wonderful looking root pie, while I go visit the widow Jem. I'm afraid I can't get out of it now, and I must leave at once." He guided Leta to a chair, picked up his muffler, and was soon gone.

Horace had never seen Leta looking so pretty. He liked the way her mind worked too, and before he knew it, they were laughing and talking together like old friends. She was also a good cook. The apple turnovers she lifted from her basket were fragrant and hot. "Smells wonderful," he said.

Leta smiled. "Horace, may I ask you something? Why are you leaving? I mean really why?"

Horace stopped eating. He had never spoken privately to her of his lost brother. "I guess because I like a challenge," he said lamely.

"Do you?" Leta said. "I hadn't noticed."

Puzzled Horace stared at her. What did she mean by that? "I don't understand," he said.

Leta stood up and walked over to the easel, her back to him. "I thought we had a friendship, before all the trouble, I mean. At the Christmas feast it seemed so in spite of Barga." Her voice was a mere whisper.

Horace sat very still. "Sit down, Leta, please. What I have to say is a long story. First I need to show you something." He removed the small carving of the broken tree from around his neck and laid it on the table between them. "It was my mother's," he began. He told Leta everything from the day he'd received the carving at his mousehood party. "So you see, I must go. I would have gone someday even if nothing else had happened. Perhaps just not so soon," he added.

Leta's eyes filled with tears. "Oh, Horace," she said.

Horace took her small paw in his own. "You are a friend. I'll always value your friendship, Leta, wherever I go."

"But I don't understand why you won't wait until spring is really here," Leta said. "The fields are deep in mud, and the weather can still change quickly. Why must you hurry?"

"Why do I need to leave now?" Horace could hardly think. He just knew he wanted to be away and on the road as soon as possible. "I can only tell you that I need to go," he said lamely. "I'll miss you all, Leta." Her paw was still in his. "You'll be getting on with your life, and that's good. Barga is a really a fine fellow at heart."

Leta withdrew her paw quickly. "Barga?" She stood up. Leta looked puzzled.

Horace felt confused. "I only meant to wish you and Barga well," he said.

Leta had turned to face him, her eyes wide with wonder. "Barga?" she said again "He's a friend, and I've never thought of him as more." Quickly she looked away from Horace, lifted her basket and flung the remains of the lunch into it. "I really must be going," she said moving toward the door. The tone of her voice sounded angry to Horace, and the slamming of the door behind her took away any doubts he might have had. Leta was angry with him.

Horace stared at the door. What did Leta mean, she'd never thought of Barga as more than a friend? He'd only meant . . . What had he meant? Worse, what had he done now?

CHAPTER 16

The portrait of Mr. Baxter was finished. Horace stood by as the colonel and Mr. Baxter inspected it. "Splendid," the colonel said, examining the painting closely. Horace had worked hard to make the picture the best he could. Horace knew he had captured something of the kindly old mouse's spirit in the gentle way his eyes seemed to look out from the painting.

Mr. Baxter served them all tea and apple cake. The colonel seated himself next to Horace. "I know about your plan to search for your brother, but what's this I hear about your leaving us any day now?" he demanded.

"I hope to leave next week," Horace said quietly.

"Hmm. So soon." The colonel took a sip of tea. "Well, so be it. But remember, should you return, you will be welcome here," he said. "And I mean that." The colonel laid a paw on Horace's shoulder. "The past is done. It is the future that matters now," he said. "If you are determined to go, then I wish you success and a safe journey."

"Thank you, sir," Horace said. He could say little more. His heart was full. It was late when he left Mr.

Baxter's. He glanced at the sand clock. In an hour curfew would start. He still had time for a walk in the garden. Without planning to, he found himself wandering
towards the north garden border. The patch of thick hosta
where Barga had arrested him and Max the night he'd
caught them looked the same. Horace settled down under
a broad leaf. In a few days he and Max would leave. Of
course, he hadn't actually told Max when yet, but he
would tomorrow. Horace rested his head in his paws.
Part of him wanted to go, knew he must go, but another
part of him wanted to stay.

A sharp voice interrupted his thoughts. "You!" It
was Barga dressed in his new captain's uniform. "Don't
tell me you're planning to cross the border again?" he
demanded.

"No, no. Nothing like that," Horace said. "I came up
here to get away. I guess to think."

Barga sat down beside him. "I've been meaning
to talk to you," he said. Horace looked at him warily.
Barga's face seemed thinner, and, though it was the same
old Barga's features, there was something else different.
"It's about that night in the rat prison," Barga said. "You
could have left me there. I'm the one who turned you in
and all. But you didn't. If it wasn't for you and Max pushing me on, I'd never have made it. I owe you."

Horace smiled. "Forget it. I guess if anyone owes anything it's me. Thanks to me the whole community nearly
came to an end. Anyway, you're a good man, Barga. I'm
glad you've got your captain's bars." Horace suddenly
knew what had changed about Barga. The old arrogance
was gone, and he liked what he saw in this new Barga.

They sat for awhile in silence until Barga said, "Look,
I know I'm a lot better at giving orders than taking them,
but I know when one of my patrol mice has something on

his mind. And right now I'd say you've got something on your mind. I'm listening if you want an ear."

"Thanks," Horace said. He looked at Barga. They could have died together back in the prison. That ought to mean something. "Barga, can I ask you something?" Horace said.

"Sure, go ahead."

"Only Max and a handful know this, but somewhere out there I have a long-lost brother, even a mother, though I doubt that she still lives or she would have come back for me." Briefly Horace told Barga the story. "So it's kind of like looking for a paw print that's years old somewhere in the wide world. Worse, if there is someone you really care for, someone you couldn't take with you, would you stay or go? I mean stay in Fleur Gardens?"

"So that's what's troubling you," Barga said. "It's Leta you're talking about." He raised a paw to hush Horace. "I've known for sometime. The truth is if it were me, I'd stay and settle down. But you aren't me, and it's something I guess only you can decide. If I could help you look for your brother, I would, but my job is here." Barga stood up. "I owe you much. I'm sorry I couldn't help you, friend," he said.

Horace said nothing for a minute. "You're right. It's up to me." He stood and extended a paw to Barga. "Thanks for listening. One day maybe I will be back."

Barga shook his paw. "You'll do okay," he said. He left before Horace could say anything more. Horace was about to leave too when he saw Leta coming along the path from the lower gardens. She waved, and Horace waved back as she walked towards him.

"Horace. I hoped you wouldn't leave without saying goodbye." She stood before him small, but straight and looking him in the eye with that clear bold look of hers.

"I'm glad you're here," Horace said. He took a deep breath. "You left in a bit of a hurry the last time I saw you. Please hear me out. Leta, if I could stay I would. I'll miss you and the others," he added quickly.

"I'll miss you too, Horace." Leta smiled. "Perhaps I ought to come along with you just to keep you and Max out of mischief."

Horace turned his head for a moment. When he looked back at Leta he thought he saw a tear in her eye. "Leta, the dangers outside are real. You know how real. You and Aunt Hanna lost everything once, and now you're happy here. I don't even know where I'm going."

"Stay then, Horace. You can paint and teach here. There's so much to be done, to learn," Leta urged. Her eyes misted. "Horace, I know you want to search for your brother and your mother, but that all happened so long ago. Surely if they lived they would have come here somehow." She touched his arm gently. "Suppose your mother never found him. She would have come back for you. And even if your brother lives, he may not remember anything about you in his new life. You were both babies when the fire happened. Oh, Horace, how will you ever find him?"

Horace stepped back. "I don't know how. I only know I have to try."

Leta smiled up at him. "Then you've chosen. I wish you well. Maybe one day you'll come back. I'd like to think that." She began walking. "I'd best be going. Good night, Horace."

"Let me walk you back to the tunnel," Horace pleaded.

"No thanks. I'd better hurry."

With a heavy heart Horace watched her go.

Curfew hadn't sounded yet, but Horace headed back to his own quarters anyway. Inside the tunnel he nearly stumbled over two small forms chasing each other. The widow Jem's oldest child grabbed his younger brother and wrestled him to the ground almost on top of Horace. "It's mine," yelled the oldest. "You give it back."

"What exactly is it you two are fighting about enough to knock an old friend over?" Horace separated the two youngsters and held each firmly by an arm.

"Take it," the youngest cried. "I didn't want that old broken thing anyway." He threw something from his chubby paw, something white. It landed at Horace's feet.

Horace stared at it unbelieving. Letting go of the two, he picked up the small carving of a broken tree. Hardly daring to breathe he slipped his own carving from his neck and placed it next to the one in his hand. It fit perfectly. "Where did you get this?" he demanded of the oldest, who stood staring at him.

"I didn't steal it, honest." The youngster's eyes were wide. "I found it. I did. It was by the east gate right where the big rat's body was. I think it must have fallen off his neck or something in the fighting. See here, where the leather tie is broken." He pointed to the broken lace that held the carving.

"Tell me how you know it belonged to the rat," Horace asked sternly.

"I saw it lying there right where he'd been just after I saw the patrol drag his body out the east gate."

"You were there?" Horace asked in surprise.

"We were both watching," the youngest piped up. "Only I can't tell you our secret hiding place."

Horace smiled briefly. "I won't ask you to tell me that. But listen to me. This is most important." He bent to show the youngsters the two carvings in his paw that now made one whole tree. "You see how they fit. I've been hoping to find this second piece. But you are absolutely certain the rat had it?"

"Hate to tell you," the oldest said, "but there were large dark rat hairs stuck in the knot where the leather had broken. I took 'em all out. Smelled like rat too. I had to wash the carving good before I could get the rat smell off it."

"So my brother's half of the tree has been around the neck of some rat for who knows how long?" Horace straightened up. "I think you two deserve a reward for finding this. If you'll walk with me, I've a nice collection of marbles you may be interested in swapping for this. They're quite fine marbles." Wide-eyed the youngsters followed. Horace delivered the marbles and waved the two on their way home.

Inside he placed the tree parts side by side on the table. "What happened to you, brother?" he whispered. "I can't believe you would give up your half of something so precious without a fight." Was the journey to find his brother over before it had even begun? Horace leaned his head on his arms and for a long time sat staring at the small delicately carved tree.

He would never know now for certain what had happened. In the morning he would tell Max and Leta.

CHAPTER 17

Horace laid the two pieces of the carving on Mr. Baxter's kitchen table. Max bent close to examine it. Leta gasped. "They fit perfectly," she said.

"So they do," Mr. Baxter agreed. "From what you've told us, Horace, I fear your search is over." His kind old face wore a look of sadness.

Horace placed the two broken parts of the tree in a small cloth bag and drew the drawstring tight. "Now what do I do?" He already knew what he would do even as he looked around at his friends.

Leta spoke first. "Stay, Horace. You can contribute so much. You and Max."

Mr. Baxter's eyes shone and his voice sounded eager. "Think of it, Horace. For the first time the future mice of Fleur Gardens will know what their ancestors really looked like, what it was like to live here. You can record it all in pictures! You can hold classes, teach the young ones how to paint."

"But I've already told the colonel that Max and I are going." Horace turned to face Max. "What about you, Max? You've been planning all along to go."

Max's face turned unexpectedly red. "You know I gave my word I'd come with you, mate. And so I would, only not alone this time. Ahem, I've a change of plans myself. You see, Miss Bea and I, well, seems like she plans on cooking for me for the rest of my life."

"How wonderful" Leta exclaimed. "But I shall sorely miss you both."

The grin on Max's face told Horace he'd already made up his mind that the two of them were going to come with him. He swallowed hard. "I didn't dream, I mean . . . why that's great, Max!" Horace couldn't stop his words from tumbling out. "But now that I've found my brother's half of the ivory tree, I guess things have changed. What I mean is you're free, Max, to stay right here and settle. I'm sure that would be best for you and Miss Bea."

Max looked grim. "Don't count on our settling here. We talked it over, and we both plan on going along with you, if you're still going."

Horace said quickly, "Max, you need to take time and think about it, and so do I. We can talk later." He tried to smile, but it felt more like a grin to him. Things would never be the same now. He and Max traveling together, free to go anywhere was one thing, but Max and Miss Bea was another.

Mr. Baxter laughed and said, "One thing is certain. The colonel has agreed to a feast of thanksgiving for our community's recovery from all the recent illness and our safe deliverance from our enemies. It will be a grand night of celebration, and I expect you all to be there." He glanced at the sand clock and uttered a groan. "Oh dear, I promised the widow Jem I wouldn't be late. She makes the best herb pies, and I'm off to learn her secret recipe." He smiled broadly and left. Horace, too, asked to be excused and left quickly. He would stay for the celebration, but after that he knew what he had to do.

Mr. Baxter had again insisted that Horace and Max join the choir for the special event. Horace would do his part and then quietly leave. "Stand still," Aunt Hanna commanded. She bent once more to fix a pin in Horace's new sash. "There that fits just fine," she said. She slipped the silky material off Horace and folded it into her work basket. "I'll sew that up tonight and tomorrow evening when you wear it you will blend right in with the rest of the singers." Her kindly face beamed.

Horace smiled weakly. "Thanks, Aunt Hanna."

Aunt Hanna gave him a motherly look. "It appears to me you look a bit peaked. You try some of that chamomile tea I've left warming in your sand pit. Get a good night's rest too." She patted his shoulder and left.

In the morning Horace woke to a startling thought. This was the day he would leave Fleur Gardens. Hastily he drank a cup of tea, ate an apple muffin, and left. The community hall was full. Every housewife in the tunnel seemed to be there helping with the feast. Leta smiled when she saw him. "I need to see you, Leta," Horace said.

Leta followed him outside into the tunnel. "If you want to talk, we'll have to find a quiet spot in the great hall." No one was in the great hall, the large meeting room built into one of the tunnels.

Horace faced Leta and took her paws in his own. "Leta, I need to tell you the truth." Leta's eyes opened wide. Horace hurried on. "I thought I was willing to stay here in Fleur Gardens, but I can't. I have to go. I may never find my brother or my mother. I believe that now, but there's a part of me that needs to try. Maybe another part of me wants to see the world out there, paint more pictures. I'm not sure." He heard her gasp.

"I know the outside world better than any of you," she cried. "None of you has ever been there. I can help, Horace. Max and Bea are going aren't they? Please understand, Horace, I want to come with you all."

"You don't understand," Horace said. "I'm not going with Max and Bea. After the celebration tonight I'll leave before anyone discovers I'm gone. It's the best thing I can do for Max. He'll be free then, really free to stay here where he belongs."

"You're going alone?" Leta's voice was almost a whisper.

"Yes, tonight," Horace said. "I've made up my mind."

Leta turned to go. "If there is no stopping you then, go if you must. I have to get back now."

Horace watched her leave. How the rest of the day went, he barely noticed. He dressed in time and hurried to take his place in the main garden court shortly after the all-clear for overground sounded. The guests were already gathering. The gardens were heavy with early lilies, fat crocuses, yellow daffodils, and sweet smells that made his whiskers tingle. Mr. Baxter stood under a canopy of fern waiting to direct the choir. Horace took his place next to Max, who winked at him. When the songs were finished, Mr. Baxter spoke words of thanksgiving that once again the community was safe and all had recovered from the sickness among them. Next the colonel spoke briefly, and finally all were welcomed to the grand feast.

Tables had been set up in the great tunnel meeting hall. Piles of cakes, pies, seeds, cherry tea, and steaming dishes, whose names Horace didn't know, were spread everywhere. Mr. Baxter gave a toast, which was soon followed by another until the room was filled with merriment.

The hour was late when guests began leaving. Horace slipped away among them.

He waited until he was sure there was no one in the tunnels. The sand clock read almost dawn when he closed his door behind him and walked swiftly to the east gate. The guard nodded to Horace, opened the gate, and stood aside. "You'll be wanting to head for the woods soon," the guard said. "It doesn't do to be out in the open once daylight comes."

"Thank you. I'll remember that," Horace said. He walked briskly, skirting the road to the north and east towards the woods. The trunks of the trees were still black, though streaks of light were beginning to turn the sky a pale pink. He could smell spring in the air. Here in the great outdoors it felt to Horace like no other spring he had ever known. Safe under the cover of thick undergrowth, he slowed his pace. *No need to hurry*, he told himself. His only goal was to make it through the woods to the hills beyond by nightfall. He had nothing solid to go on that would make him choose to go north, only the slimmest hope of finding some traces of his lost family, but it seemed his best choice at the moment.

Once or twice he thought he heard footsteps, or something like them, and stopped to listen. But each time he stopped, he heard nothing more than the morning noises of birds. At midday he halted to eat a light lunch near a small stream. He bent to scoop water into his cup when a sound from behind startled him. Horace grabbed his backpack from the ground and turned ready to defend himself against who or whatever it was. The backpack dropped from his paws.

"What are you doing here?" Horace demanded. Not two feet away stood Leta. With her backpack, she looked prepared for a long hike. Her eyes sparkled as she threw the backpack down and plopped onto the ground.

"I'll walk you back," Horace said.

"If you do, I'll leave again as soon as you turn your back," Leta said in a determined voice. "And just how long do you think you can keep taking me back?"

Horace picked up his pack and began walking north. He didn't look behind him, but he could hear her footsteps. He kept going hoping she would soon be discouraged. Finally when he could stand it no longer, he stopped and faced her. "You know I can't take you, Leta."

"But you're not taking me. I'm coming all on my own," she insisted. "But I do admit I wouldn't mind company." She sat down and removed her backpack. "You did say you would take me if you could. Well, now you can."

Horace sat down beside her. "It's too dangerous," he said. Leta handed him a cold pasty and took out one for herself. Horace took a bite. "All I know is that I'm heading north, and I can't take you," he said.

Leta took a folded map from her pack. "North, that's good. Mr. Baxter thought you might be since he told you the rat who wore your brother's symbol may have come from the north. There were rats from the north who migrated to the park the year after your mother left you at Fleur Gardens."

"He told you that?" Horace looked at her sharply. "And the map, did he give that to you also?" She nodded and handed him the map. Horace shook his head. "So, I take it he knew you were coming?"

Leta took another bite of pasty before she answered. "Hmm. Yes, and Aunt Hanna too. She sent these along just in case you'd forgotten lunch."

Horace stared at her. "Next you'll tell me Max knew and will be coming right along any time now." He flipped open the map. The writing was Mr. Baxter's. "*You'll be wanting, this*," he read. "*It should help you find your way through the north hills, my old homeland.*" At the bottom he had signed it, "*Affectionately, Your friend, Mr. Baxter.*" Horace looked at Leta questioningly.

"I haven't told you about Max yet," she said. "If I had a sand clock, I would say they ought to catch up with us in a couple of hours."

Horace swung around to search the woods behind them. "You told him, didn't you!" Anger filled him.

Leta shook the crumbs from her lap. "Yes, and I'd do it again." She stood to her feet, tears filling her eyes. "Do you think you can just run off and leave those who love you behind? Do you think you're the only one who is brave enough, noble enough to leave Fleur Gardens? Well, you're not," she cried.

Horace stood dumbfounded. He opened his mouth to say something but Leta interrupted. "Do you think mice live wherever their hearts desire for nothing? The world is full of us, and always will be. Fleur Gardens is special, but we've had our time there. Think of it, Horace, wherever we go, we'll take all of that with us in our hearts forever."

"It won't be easy," Horace said. "You and Aunt Hanna know the dangers."

Leta touched his paw lightly. "Yes, I know, but sometimes the best things come out of the hard times. Sharing them helps."

Horace drew a deep breath. "So, you think you've convinced me," he said. "I'll have to think about it." The look on Leta's face was almost more than he could bear, but he pretended not to notice. Instead, he reached into his pack and drew out the small bag that held one broken half of the ivory tree. Carefully he placed the symbol around Leta's neck. Reaching under his neck fur he held out the other matching half. "Now, miss," he said. "I've thought about it, and unless you change your mind, I plan

not to lose you for as long as you wear your half of the tree, and I wear mine."

Leta held the small carving between her paws. "Oh, Horace, this was your brother's—the half of the ivory that will always be his—and I am honored to wear it."

Horace looked down at his own part of the white tree. "I'm glad you're the one wearing the other half now." He slipped the ivory under his fur. "Somehow I know that my father must have given this to my mother before she broke it to save her children. We may never find out." He turned away and began picking up the remains of their lunch. "I suppose if Max and Miss Bea are as determined as you to go along, we'd better look for them."

Leta turned back to look at the path they'd come along. "The woods are so thick and grand," she said. "Living at Fleur Gardens, I'd almost forgotten all this."

Horace stood at her side. "Spring seems to be alive when you see it like this." The quiet of the forest surrounded them like a hush, almost too quiet. Horace felt uneasy. This wasn't Fleur Gardens, it was far more dangerous. Low gray clouds were beginning to gather, and the morning sun had disappeared.

The sudden shout of a familiar voice broke the silence. "Ahoy, mate," Max cried as he came into sight. Beside him walked Miss Bea, and behind her Mr. Baxter, looking as cheerful as ever. There was strength in their stride, joy on their faces.

"Mr. Baxter," Horace cried. "I don't understand." He glanced down at Leta, but she too wore a look of utter surprise.

Mr. Baxter smiled and sat down to rest. "Now, my boy, it's about time this old storyteller moved on. I've a good many stories left in me and a feeling in my whiskers that somewhere out there are mousefolks willing to listen. It makes me feel young again. Besides I like the idea of seeing my old home territory again."

Horace felt his own whiskers twitching. He struggled to find words. "Max, Mr. Baxter, Miss Bea, I don't know what to say." Swallowing hard, he began again. "I don't deserve any of you. But if you can put up with me, then I do say that no mouse could ever have better company or finer friends."

Max clapped a heavy paw on Horace's shoulder. "And that's not all, mate, no indeed. You've also got yourself the best cook in mousedom," he said with a wink at Miss Bea.

Horace grinned then looked anxiously at Mr. Baxter, who sat resting against a stone. "We don't have to push on," he said. "If you like, sir, we can stay the night right here."

"Not at all. I'm ready and glad to be on the move," Mr. Baxter answered quickly. He rose to his feet and lifted his pack. "Lead the way, my boy."

Max hoisted his own pack into place. "And just which way are we to go, mate?" he asked, looking at Horace expectantly. "Whatever your plan is, we're all of us ready and willing to follow. And, if I don't miss my guess, we're in for a bit of rain," he added.

Horace felt his face grow warm. If only he had a real plan. "We go north. That's it. Straight north," he replied trying to sound confident.

It wasn't a plan exactly, but at least it was a direction, and for now it would have to do. Max was right too about the coming rain, Horace's whiskers had already begun to sense a dampness in the air.

 **CHAPTER 18**

Horace called a halt. For two days gray skies and light showers had followed them as they walked north. At night they'd stopped to camp under thick pine branches low to the ground. Now the rain fell in hard straight lines, soaking everything and making it difficult to see ahead. Thick mud oozed above their paws. In some places pools of water spread above the sodden ground, forcing them to go around before they could continue north. A gust of wind whipping through the branches of the great oak above Horace sent a sudden deluge of water onto the travelers. "We can't keep going in this," he said, "we have to find shelter." All of them were soaked, dirty, and weary. Even Miss Bea's cheerful face looked bleak. Leta's drenched cloak clung to her.

Mr. Baxter wiped his face. "Well," he said, "a dry log would be welcome right now." He closed his eyes for a moment then opened them wide. "Why don't I just leave my pack here and take a look? There must be a fallen tree around here somewhere."

Horace slid his pack from his shoulders. "You're prob-ably right about the log," he said. "We've been following an old animal path until now, but farther into the trees is the place to look. I'll go."

Max, who'd been standing by listening, spoke up. "Not meaning to brag, mate," he said, "but I've done a bit of scouting in my day. Besides, you've led the way all day. I'll go. You all stay here and be ready to sing out so I can find you again."

Horace gripped his friend's shoulder. "I'll trust your skills then, but be careful out there, Max." With a weary sigh he let go and slumped back against the rough bark of the tree. He'd led them all into a mess, and for what? He looked at Leta seated next to Miss Bea; the two of them were close to exhaustion. They should all have been back in Fleur Gardens, not in this wilderness.

How long they'd sat under the oak Horace didn't know. The rain continued harder than ever, and he shivered in the cold. Leta and Miss Bea huddled together under a small piece of canvas from Mr. Baxter's pack. Max's shout brought them all quickly to their feet. Horace shouted back, "Over here, Max. We're over here." Leta and Miss Bea, wide awake now, joined their cries to his.

Water streamed down Max's face as he hurried towards them. He was not alone. Two young field mice came behind him. "Rax and Tor," Max explained quickly. "Found them foraging not a quarter-mile from here. We can spend the night at their place," he said reaching for his backpack. The two strangers took Miss Bea's pack and Leta's, hoisting them to their shoulders.

The thought of shelter and a good meal made the heavy pack on Horace's back almost bearable as he followed the strangers. When at last their guides stopped, Horace stared in dismay. An ancient cabin, its roof fallen in, its log walls sagging and weed covered, stood in front of them. "Anybody home?" called Tor.

From the doorless entry a great cheerful voice boomed in answer. "Come in and bring your guests with you." A round-bellied, gray whiskered mouse strode into view. In spite of his years, he spoke with vigor. "Travellers caught out in this northeaster from the looks of you. Come in. Get yourselves dry and have some of Mrs. Took's hot grog to warm you." As he waved them in, Horace saw that a dozen or so others were gathering, and behind them still more appeared. "Welcome to Field Manor, home of the Tooks clan. J. P. Dominick Took at your service." He extended a paw to Mr. Baxter, and then to each. Youngsters eager to see pressed against the visitors. Mr. Took shooed them back. "Off with you for now. Tonight you can join your elders and hear our friends' stories. Off you go."

Horace turned to thank their host and give formal introductions for himself and his party in the way of mousedom custom everywhere. While they had been meeting the elder Tooks, fathers and mothers, aunts and uncles and cousins, and trying to note who was who, Rax and Tor quietly slipped away with their baggage. They returned with trays of acorn cups steaming with the spicy smell of sweet mint.

Mrs. Took had stood by her husband beaming her delight as they chatted. Horace was certain that few travelers passed this way, and so their coming was indeed an event. After a while Leta sneezed. Immediately Mrs. Took's face changed. "Oh, mercy me," she cried. "How could we keep you standing here wet as you are? Now you just come with me, dearies, and get dry."

Horace couldn't help thinking of Fleur Gardens and its tunnels as Mrs. Took led them behind fallen beams and rotted boards to the nests. The nests were warm and dry, and there were many of them hidden in the old cabin. Their back packs were waiting for them, and fresh straw pallets laid nearby. With a sigh Horace dismissed all thoughts of Fleur Gardens and turned to the present. "The Field Manor it is, and I may as well get used to such from now on."

By nightfall, warmed and well fed on corn cakes and wheat-berry pies washed down with wildberry-mint tea, Horace felt the great hall of the cabin seemed a cheery place after all. A mouse fireplace of fieldstones sparkled with the light of a good husk fire. The large family of Tooks made the room even warmer as they crowded together. For a long while their host, affectionately called Grand-J, gave the history of the family and how the first Tooks had come to the Manor. Then a robust farmer mouse stood to describe the beginnings of Took farms, ending on the happy note that this year's early spring start meant a grand harvest could be expected. All of this was interrupted time and again with cheers or words of encouragement.

Then it was Mr. Baxter's turn as the eldest among the visitors. He began with a brief mention of the nests they'd left in the great park. Horace glanced over at Max and Miss Bea, and then at Leta. All of them had agreed to say nothing of Fleur Gardens or its great advancements. It would not do to speak of such things to those who had no idea of them.

"All this rain," said Mr. Baxter, "reminds me of a flood not so very long ago. Shall I tell you the story of how it saved a whole community of mice from certain capture by a nearby rat clan?"

Cries of "Yes, yes, tell us that story" rang out from rows of eager young mice seated in front of their elders.

Mr. Baxter smiled. "It is one of my favorites," he said. "Now this is how it all came about."

As he told the story, Horace remembered every detail. It was his story and Max's. At the end one youngster cried out, "And did all the sick paroles get better?"

Mr. Baxter smiled. "You mean the patrols who were too sick to guard the community? Yes, they most certainly did get well, and all of them joined in a grand feast of celebration." Loud applause rang as Mr. Baxter took his seat.

Grand-J Took now stood and looked directly at Horace. "Now, sir, may we hear what brings you and your company into our woods?"

Horace stood as Grand-J sat down to listen. As Horace began to speak, the room grew very still. "I fear my story is one that begins with a mystery," he said. "On the night of a great fire many years ago, my mother and my brother disappeared." No one interrupted as he told how his mother had left him in the care of Mr. Baxter at the great park and gone back to the fire area to find his brother, but never returned. Briefly he spoke of his mousehood party. "So now my friends and I travel north in hope that we may yet find some answers to what happened after the great fire." For a few moments silence filled the hall except for a sigh or a mournful sniffle here and there.

Then from his place by the fire, the oldest mouse Horace had ever seen, his voice creaking said, "It was in the summer Bran Took lost his tail to a night owl when a sad company of refugees passed this way. I was but a lad then." His voice grew faint. He coughed, cleared his throat, and went on. "I recall talk about a fire, a great one. But the survivors who came through our field were soon gone from here. Others followed them, all headed north, my boy. It is all I remember." After that the old one fell silent and seemed either asleep or lost in thought.

"It must have been the same fire," Leta said. Her eyes were bright with excitement. "We know now that they came this way. And we know they went north. Your family could have been with them."

Horace stared but said nothing. Leta might be right. His brother could have stopped at this very manor hall!

Mr. Baxter held up his paw. "Remember it was a long time ago that these things happened. We cannot be sure it was the very fire that brought you to us, Horace, though it may have indeed been."

Horace at last found his voice. "All the same, the old one said north, and that is where we have been heading all this while. It is almost as if this were a sign."

"Well, mate," Max declared, "we're with you whichever way the wind blows. That is to say, north it is then." He lowered his voice, "Listening to you made the old fellow remember something. Though I wouldn't be certain he hasn't mixed a few details you gave him in with his memories. Still, it's more to go on then we've had before, I say."

"We'll leave in the morning," Horace stated. "Grand-J says from the feel of his bones the weather ought to be changing for the better." Horace glanced up as Mrs. Took approached carrying a tray of corn pasties. He smiled. The motherly mouse had seen to it that all her guests were treated to every good thing the cooks of Field Manor had to offer. Though nothing like the grand feasts of Fleur Gardens, the food was plentiful and wholesome. If his mission were not now so urgent, he would have liked to stay on awhile and paint a few portraits. All about him were faces old and young that made his paws itch to take up a pencil and begin to sketch.

That night while the others slept, Horace drew a picture in his sketch pad. When he was through, he tore out the page, rolled it carefully, and tied it with a bit of string.

Moving softly he placed the scroll in the empty hall near the fireplace where the old man had sat. "Someone will find it and give it to the old fellow," he whispered. It should please him to see a sketch of himself. Horace slept well the rest of the night.

CHAPTER 19

Blue sky and a bright sun shone above the travelers as they headed north. Once they were out of sight of Field Manor, the forest ahead grew thick with tangled berry bushes, creeper vines, and many kinds of trees, some of them old and of a great size. Horace, who'd seemed lost in thought most of the day, hardly noticed that the others were beginning to lag behind until Max held up his paw to signal a halt. "Don't know about you, mate, but these two fair mouse-maids are about worn out. What do you say we make camp for the night?"

Horace felt his face grow warm as he looked back at Leta and Miss Bea. "I'm sorry," he said. "We ought to have stopped before this. The sun's almost down. Don't know where my mind is, Max." Horace slid his backpack to the ground. For the last several hours he'd gone over and over in his mind what might lie ahead. He glanced at the thick pines and the natural shelter formed by their long sweeping branches that almost touched the ground. "This will do nicely for tonight," he said. The thick carpet of pine needles underfoot would at least make for comfortable beds.

While Mr. Baxter and Horace made a campfire, Max disappeared into the woods. He returned to camp with an armful of fiddlehead ferns. Miss Bea was stirring a pot of soup slung on poles over the open fire. She beamed at Max. "If I had time and a bit of acorn flour, I'd mix up some fiddlehead cakes, but these will do fine to flavor our soup."

Mr. Baxter praised the soup's grand flavor as the finest he could remember. And though there was plenty, not a drop remained in Miss Bea's pot. The small fire glowed as darkness fell, and night sounds of the woods began. It was not long after the meal before one by one the tired travelers rolled into their blankets for sleep. Horace watched the fire and listened to the soft breathing sounds of the others. He wished for sleep, but it was long before it came.

The days of hard hiking that followed toughened their paws, but the farther north they went the more barren and forbidding the way became. Now the rock-strewn hill before them with its little vegetation seemed impassible. Max returned from scouting ahead with a glum look on his face. "No way around it," he stated. "Swamp ground on one side with no end to it in sight, and a black river on the other. The current is too swift to try to cross, and there are enough boulders to make rafting dangerous. We'll have to climb."

Horace nodded. He'd already noted a sort of narrow winding path, though it looked steep in places. The rest was sheer-faced rock. They would have to take their chances on the path.

"I'll go first," he ordered, "then Leta, Mr. Baxter, Miss Bea, and Max, you bring up the rear. Once I'm up top, I'll find something to fasten a rope line to, and I'll lower it down to help you climb."

As Horace climbed, stones skidded under his paws, and the hard ground gave him few places to find holds. Here and there he grasped the branch of a bush struggling to live in the harsh conditions. He was almost there. If he could just reach the small ledge above, he'd be nearly to the top. The soft swishing sound of something whizzing close to his ear made him look up. Stunned, he stared at the two figures above him.

Two young mice held strung bows pointed at Horace. "Halt where you are," one commanded. "Who are you and what are you doing here?" Their faces were grim, the look in their eyes stern.

Horace swallowed hard. Most likely they'd already seen the others below. "Travelers hoping to find our way north," he replied. "I'd explain a whole lot better if you'd let me up onto the ledge. Ground's not too stable here," he said as a stone under his paw slid away.

"Grab hold," the youth who seemed in charge ordered, lowering the end of his bow to Horace. Though he worried that the slender bow might not be that sturdy, Horace had little choice but to grasp it. At the same time he pushed himself forward and found himself on the ledge with two strong paws supporting him. "You'll stay put until we get the rest of your party up, and then we'll see what the elders have to say when we take you before the council," the youth said. Puzzled, Horace wanted to ask what was going on, but the two mice had turned their attention to lowering a thick vine over the ledge. Horace went to lend a paw.

Breathing hard and barely able to stand, Leta was the first to make it to the ledge. "Thank you," she murmured as Horace led her away from the edge. From the ledge to the top of the hill above them was sheer rock. They could never have climbed to the top. But a little ways from the ledge, almost hidden by a jutting rock was the opening to a cave. Leta leaned against the rock grate-fully. "Whoever our friends are," she said, "I'm glad they came along just when they did." She glanced above her and then at Horace. "They must have come through that cave," she said with a shudder.

Horace frowned. "Yes, I think it has to lead to the other side, but there's something you need to know, Leta. They aren't exactly our friends. They seem suspicious of us now that we've stumbled into their territory." Leta looked back at the strangers who were helping Mr. Baxter stand. Miss Bea was already up and lending her own paw to steady the vine as Max reached for the ledge. In a few moments all of them were ushered into the opening of the cave.

"I say, what's all this about a council?" Max de-manded.

Mr. Baxter patted Max's shoulder. In a low voice he said, "I believe these two are pretty new to mousehood and a bit overzealous. They've probably been told to be on the lookout for any possible danger to the commu-nity." He smiled. "Reminds me of some other youngsters I've known in my day."

Horace felt his whiskers tingle. Youngsters or not, he didn't like the sound of a council, and he didn't like the ever-winding cave tunnels they were passing through. He was about to demand an explanation when the narrow entry they'd entered ended in a wide cavern. A reception committee awaited them. In fact, it looked as if the whole community had turned out to greet them.

Their guides stopped in front of two elderly mice seated on a raised platform of rock. The guide next to Horace bowed slightly. "Madam," he said, "we found these mice trying to scale the cliff. Claims they're travel-ing north," he added pointing to Horace.

Quickly Horace spoke up. "That's right, madam. We are travelers and grateful for your help."

"What brings you north?" the old mouse asked. The elder mouse beside her seemed nearly asleep, his head drooped low on his chest until a sudden snore brought him awake.

Horace continued speaking. "We are searching for a party of refugees who passed this way a long time ago. They fled after their homes were destroyed by fire. We know only that they came north. My own brother and mother may have been with them." Horace was about to introduce the others, but before he could, the old one interrupted him.

"You need search no farther," she said. "I believe we are the refugees you seek. What is your name?" All eyes turned to Horace, who had gone quite pale. Stumbling for words Horace told her. Whispers and sighs rose among the crowd of mice.

"Then I fear the news is not good," the old one said. "On the night of the great fire many families were scattered. Some perished; others too young to care for themselves were snatched to safety by strangers fleeing the scene. There was no turning back. When your mother came searching for your brother, she found him here, but she would not stay with us. She was anxious to return for the son she had left behind. Rumors had come to us of armies of rats on the move, even close to these cliffs, and few pathways were safe. I fear your mother and brother perished." Her voice struck a deadly pain into Horace.

"Oh, Horace, I am so sorry," Leta cried. Tears filled her eyes. Miss Bea clasped her close and the two wept.

The old one spoke more softly now, as she held up her paw. "We shall not speak more now. You are weary from your travels. We will see to your refreshment and comfort such as we have to give." She had already turned to two of her aides to give instructions for the guests, but Horace's mind raced with unanswered questions.

How did she know his mother and brother were dead? What proof was there? What about his brother's necklace and the rat who was wearing it? He needed more than the old ones' words. As the little group was ushered to an adjoining tunnel, Horace turned back. "We thank you for your hospitality, madam. But we will be leaving in the morning."

"As you wish," the old one said. "You are surely eager to return to your homes."

"Not at all, madam" Horace said firmly. "We will press north. It may be that some trace of my family remains yet to find."

"Many dangers await you. Heed my words and return home. No one is safe in the world, not even here, though we keep vigilant watch." Horace did not answer. "I see," she continued, "that you are determined to go on. You will need your rest." With a nod of her head she dismissed him.

The guest nest was nothing like those at Fleur Gardens. Bare, cold stone walls surrounded them. The dried grasses of the beds provided little warmth. Settling down in his blanket Max observed, "There's little in the way of comfort for these poor blokes. Seems like they moved into these old cave tunnels the way they were and left them that way. Could do with a few improvements, I say. Suppose if we were to hang about for awhile we could teach them a few tricks from Fleur Gardens, eh mate?"

"No doubt," Horace replied. He turned his face to the wall and said no more. Why did these mice stay in such cold bleak caves? Only a few days march away, the forests were green and full of places that would have made better quarters.

As if reading Horace's thoughts, Mr. Baxter, said, "There is much fear here. I wouldn't doubt but what the elders have kept alive the worst memories of the past and little more. Why else should a band of refugees choose to retreat into such a wilderness place? Fear is a terrible master. I believe the young ones have never known anything better than these cold caves." Silence followed and then light snoring sounds.

Horace was sleeping soundly when a light touch on his shoulder woke him. Startled, he looked up into the face of one of the guards. "Be quiet and come with me," he said. Alert and wary, Horace rose and followed the young mouse, who led him past the great cavern down a narrow tunnel and from there into the pale light of dawn. The old mouse, heavily wrapped against the morning chill, stood waiting for them.

"There is something I must show you," she said. "It has to do with your mother. Come." Without another word she turned and led the way downhill. The path on this north side of the hill sloped gently to the forest floor below. At the foot of the hill she motioned to the guard. "Stay here until I return." The forest ahead lay deep in shadows just beginning to be touched by the pale morning light. They followed an old animal path. Afraid of what they would find, Horace walked silently.

Where the path forked, they turned left and followed it deeper into the forest. When they had walked a good ways, Horace saw the object of their search. Close to the path under a low pine was a grave marked by a large smooth rock. The outline of a slender paw scratched upon the rock was the only sign that this was no ordinary stone. His eyes full of questions, Horace looked at the old mouse.

"I was wrong not to tell you at once, but this is your mother's grave" she said. "Since you are determined to

go north, I could not let you go without telling you. Your mother was killed by rats moving through the area." Horace only stared at her. "Not long after she left us, my husband and I came this far to forage. We found her wounded and near death, lying in the woods. It was already too late to save her. Her last words were 'Save my son.' It was all she said. Close by we found clear signs that rats had been this way, and though we looked high and low we could find no trace of the young one. Your brother must have been taken by the rats." She paused as Horace covered his face. "The woods are thick, but we searched as well as we could. We buried her here before we left. It has been many years, and the pine above her has grown, but this is the place."

Horace uncovered his face. "But why didn't you rouse the others to search? What if my brother was only wounded, or had wandered off before the attack?" Anger edged Horace's voice. He knelt by his mother's grave and groaned.

The old mouse wrapped her cloak tighter. "It was a long time ago. We were afraid that the rats might return. There was no more time. We did what we could." She turned to go. "When you are ready, you are welcome to come back to us. We will help you down the other side of the cliff so that you may go back to your home."

"I will not go back. We go north," Horace said.

"Stay here then," the old mouse ordered. "I will send the others to join you."

Horace did not see her go. Everything pointed to the truth of what she had told him, even how a rat came to be wearing his brother's necklace. He had surely found his mother, but what had happened to his brother? How could he be certain his brother had died? Maybe he'd lost the necklace and some rat had found it. He could have wandered off to another place. And maybe he too was dead. Tears ran down his face. When the others finally came, Horace no longer wept. His voice did not waver as he told them all the old mouse had said.

Mr. Baxter gripped Horace's shoulder. "Had your mother lived, she would have found her way back to Fleur Gardens. Surely you were meant to find this place. Who knows what may lie ahead? But we've come this far, and if you are ready to press on, we will go together." He paused then said. "Bless me, but I feel it in my bones. There is a purpose in this."

They had left the cliff far behind them when Max said, "Well, mate, if there are many more places like our cliff dwellers. I say there's a great lot to be done in this world yet. Poor blokes. Makes my paws itch to show them a thing or two about tunnels. A few improvements would take some of the harshness out of their lives."

"Yes, and some good stories might ease their fears," added Mr. Baxter.

Horace couldn't feel pity for the old one or her people. Not now. He could only think of one thing—had his brother died too or been captured? Would they ever find out?

 **CHAPTER 20**

Horace reached out to steady Leta as she tripped over a root. Three days of walking had brought them into thick woods. Leta stood still for a moment and drew a deep breath. "Aunt Hanna used to say, 'Keep north. Watch for the bushy growth on pines, spruces, hemlocks, and soft woods, and that will be the south side,' but it seems like the roots in here turn every way, and who can tell what side has more growth?"

"True," Horace agreed and added, "but you'll note the bark of poplar trees is whitest on the south side and darkest on the north side, and that's a good compass."

Ahead of them Max chimed in, "Right, mate, and don't forget your anthills. Won't find them on the north, just on the south side of trees or rocks."

"Give me a patch of pilotweed," Miss Bea sang out, "and I'll tell you north and south from its leaves. Though can't say I've seen any of those bright yellow flowers around here."

Late in the afternoon, Mr. Baxter who'd been un-usually quiet stood still and raised his hand in signal. "Listen," he said. "Hear it? It sounds like singing. Bless me, someone is singing—a song I know well. Praise be!" With a glad look on his face he hurried forward.

"Hold on," Horace called trying not to shout. "We don't know what's ahead." But it was too late. Mr. Baxter had already disappeared into a thicket of pines. As he hurried after him, Horace did hear the faint sounds of singing.

All of them stared in amazement as they reached the edge of a clearing that had been hidden by the pines. In its center stood the oldest, widest oak Horace had ever seen. Nestled in its spreading roots doors and windows had been carved into the great trunk. Mr. Baxter was talking excitedly to an elderly mouse dressed in a long robe tied about the middle with a simple rope. "Welcome to Oak Abbey of the gray-friars," the old one said. A door in the abbey opened as two more friars appeared to greet them.

Mr. Baxter's face beamed as he turned to Horace and the others. "Come, meet Brother Barnabas. Long ago I had heard the stories of such places as this, but never dreamed of one day seeing one for myself."

Brother Barnabas laughed heartily and extended both paws to the travelers. "Greetings!" he said. "You are all welcome to our little community." Turning to the two brothers who had joined him, he introduced them. "This is Brother John," he said indicating a gray mouse who looked about the same good age as himself. "And this is Brother Luke, our herbalist." The heavyset mouse smiled broadly at his name. "Also our chief cook, I might add," Brother Barnabas said and chuckled heartily. At the sound of someone hurrying toward them, Brother Barnabas glanced back. "Ah, Brother Timothy, come meet our guests."

As the young mouse named Timothy came striding towards the group, Horace felt his heart leap. Brother

Timothy had stopped, and he too stood staring at Horace. Mr. Baxter, Max, Leta, and Miss Bea were speechless. It was Brother Barnabas who broke the silence. "I say, you two do look much alike. I have heard of such rare wonders! Brother Timothy, and you, sir," he said turning to Horace, "now that I see you together, I'd say you could almost pass for one another. Timothy, my son, it looks as if there are two of you as alike as two peas in a pod." It was true almost to a whisker. "Now I wonder do any of the rest of us have someone out in the world who might pass for us?" He laughed heartily. "Surely, it is well that such a thing is rare. Come, my son, let us show our guests inside where they can freshen up before the evening meal."

The grip around Horace's heart loosened. He shook his head as if to clear it. *Son?* The young friar was the son of the old one! For a moment, Horace had hoped, no, felt certain that somehow they had stumbled upon his own brother. The likeness to himself was startling. He too knew it did happen that one face might be so like another it could be mistaken for the other. But the shock of seeing a stranger who looked so like him had left him tired and discouraged. With bent shoulders and slow steps, Horace followed the others to the Abbey. Behind the others Leta stood waiting at the door. Her eyes glistened with tears as he neared. "I'm so sorry, Horace," she said softly.

Brother Barnabas led the travelers into the main hall, a large room with long tables and benches. One wall held an enormous fireplace, and a delicious aroma of herbs and spices rose from the large cooking pots hanging above the fire. An archway led into a wide hall with several doors, one a double wooden door that stood open. The room beyond it was filled with pallets, and Horace saw that several were occupied. "In here," Brother Barnabas said, "we have our infirmary. Only a few patients need

our care at this time of year, but winter will find us full."
A frail old squirrel raised his paw weakly, and Brother
Barnabas waved back as he called, "Good evening to
you, Maximus."

On their left, further down the hall was a dormitory
where some of the brothers slept, and beyond that were
guest rooms, various storage rooms, and work rooms.
"We live a simple life here," Brother Barnabas explained,
"caring for the sick, the traveler, the gardens, and whatever else we may." With a twinkle in his eye, he chuckled
and said, "We celebrate much here, thanks to the abun-
dance of our fields. You will join us tonight at supper, but
now you must be weary, and Brother Timothy will show
you to your quarters. I will go and inform the cooks that
we shall have extra guests." He left, and the young friar
led them to the guest rooms. Miss Bea and Leta were
shown into the first room, Horace, Max, and Mr. Baxter
into the next. Horace noted the clean straw pallets and
the simple furnishings of a plain but cheerful room. He
turned to thank their guide, but Brother Timothy had already slipped away.

"Praise be," said Mr. Baxter stretching himself on one
of the pallets. "These old bones will rest well tonight," he
added. In a moment Max and Horace followed suit. No
one said more as the last rays of sun filtered through the
window to cast a gentle glow on the wooden walls.

Horace thought he must have dozed when a light
tapping at the door caught his attention. A middle-aged
mouse, who announced himself as Brother Lysias, guided
them all to the supper hall. Leta and Miss Bea were already seated at one of the long tables. Seated nearby,
several friars, two moles, a gentleman rabbit wearing a
bandage around his head, and a pair of elderly hedgehogs
waited quietly for the meal to begin. As Brother Barnabas
led them all in a song of thanks, Horace couldn't help

smiling at the raspy voices of the hedgehogs next to him.

While they ate from platters piled high with field greens, pie, corn pudding, raspberry scones, tender leaf salad with pod dressing, and pitchers of cool cherry-mint tea, Horace listened to the hedgehogs' tales of how they'd come to Oak Abbey.

The old hedgehog's voice sounded even raspier coming through mouthfuls of pie. "I sez to the missus, no better place to end our days than at the Abbey. Course, we do our share of work on the grounds and all that, long as we can." He paused for a drink of tea, swallowed, and groaned with pleasure. "Ain't many places like the Abbey, sez I."

Not even Horace could eat another bite by the time the meal was cleared. Max, too, looked content as he lifted a last spoonful of dessert. Leta and Miss Bea had finished a while ago, and Mr. Baxter was already deep in conversation with the brother seated next to him.

Brother Barnabas rose and signaled for quiet, waiting for silence before he spoke. "Now friends, may we hear how you came to our woods and where your journey leads you? We seldom hear news from outside, and we eagerly await any word you may bring."

Brother Barnabas looked at Mr. Baxter, and Mr. Baxter stood and cleared his throat. "Good brothers and company all, I thank you for your hospitality. But as to our journey, I must ask our leader to speak, for it is his story that is indeed the reason we are here." He turned and held out his paw to Horace and sat down as Horace rose.

"Well, then, the privilege is mine," Horace began, "and I, too, thank you for your kind welcome." Quietly Horace began to tell his story. As before, he made no mention of Fleur Gardens, though the effect of the warmth and peace of the Abbey nearly made him let down his guard at least once. He did speak plainly of the wretched cliff mice they'd left only days ago and had come to the part about his mother's grave and her dying wish. The room full of brothers grew suddenly quieter than it had been, almost as if none dared to make even the sound of breathing. "It was a long time ago, and my brother may indeed have been taken away by the rats or died somewhere along the way. We are heading north in the hope that even now there may yet be some clue to what happened," Horace paused. "That is the reason your son, Brother Timothy, so startled me earlier today," he said looking at Brother Barnabas. "From his looks he might indeed have been my lost brother."

Among the friars someone gasped, and then many excited voices began talking at once.

CHAPTER 21

Brother Timothy had gone quite pale when the voice of Brother Barnabas rose above the din with a cry, "Your brother! Yes, indeed it must be so." He stood to his feet as a hush fell on the room. "Young Timothy is like a son to me, and so I call him *son*. But on the day we found him, dazed from a lump on his head and wandering alone in the woods, he was no more than a mouseling." Horace gripped the table as dizziness enveloped him. Brother Barnabas went on, "Because he was so young, he could not tell us who he was or where he had come from. Though we searched far and wide, we found no traces except for signs that rats had been in the vicinity of the woods a few days journey from here. We assumed they had left him for dead, but he revived and wandered off into the woods until at last we found him. There was little else to do but bring him back to the Abbey, where he has lived among us all these years."

Mr. Baxter rose to his feet, his voice was dazed, "Twins," he cried. "All these years I never understood that your lost brother was also your twin!" He turned to Horace, "Your mother spoke of an exact replica, but I thought she meant only the two halves of the ivory necklace. Until now I did not know that she was speaking of twin brothers."

Horace choked back a sob. Across the room Brother Timothy had risen to his feet, an identical sob in his throat. It was Brother Barnabas who led the two together, and while they wept on each other's shoulder, loud cheers and claps arose in the room.

When at last Timothy and Horace were seated once more at the table, Leta removed the ivory necklace from her neck and held it out to Timothy. "This is yours now," she said. "Your mother placed this half of a single carving on each of you the night of the fire. Yours must have been stolen by the rats. It is good to know that you have it back at last."

Timothy took the carving and stared at it. Horace had removed his own piece and placed it on the table. The pieces fit together exactly to form a maple tree. Timothy held his half reverently for a moment before slipping it into the leather pouch at his waist. Turning to Mr. Baxter, he begged, "Sir, I should like to hear about the night of the great fire. What was my mother like?"

As Mr. Baxter told the story once more, Horace pictured the events of that night. A tear slid down into his whiskers. His own mother had been the bravest of mice, and had she lived, he would have wanted her to be proud of him.

Long into the night the celebration continued. Timothy and Horace talked until their voices grew raspy with weariness. Max, Miss Bea, Leta, and Mr. Baxter listening tried to fill in details of their journey, laughing and wiping tears in all the sad parts. The large room had long ago emptied of friars. The weary travelers finally retired. Horace parted from Timothy with a great hug

and assured him, that come morning, they would take up where they had left off.

In the stillness of the darkened dormitory, a figure sat looking out of the arched window at the night sky. By the time he arose, the night was far gone. In the guest room Horace, too, watched the hours pass as he lay thinking and planning. If his brother wanted to see Fleur Gardens, perhaps that would be the best course to take. Horace knew the colonel would welcome his brother and be glad to see the others return. Max's loud snoring broke into Horace's thoughts. Max, Miss Bea, Leta, and Mr. Baxter had left behind all the advantages of Fleur Gardens to help him find his brother, and now there was nothing to keep them all from returning home. Satisfied, he rolled over and slept.

Breakfast was a grand affair. The tables were piled high with apple flatcakes, pitchers of raspberry syrup, honey butter, nut meats, slabs of corn pudding, and hot rose hip tea. Brother Barnabas seated Horace and his friends together by him. The morning feast was about to begin when a tired looking Brother Timothy hurried in to sit across from Horace.

Timothy piled his plate high with corn pudding. "One of my favorite foods," he explained passing the plate to Horace. Horace grinned. It was one of his favorites too. Maybe liking the same foods was a twin thing. Only one thing they could not agree on.

For an hour after finishing the morning meal Horace and Brother Timothy had argued. "But I've only just found you," Horace said. "Brother Barnabas and the friars have been good to care for you all this time, but now we have each other," he insisted. "If you don't want to go to Fleur Gardens, we can go elsewhere, settle in a new place, make a new life." Horace paused to look at the others standing close by. "We're all in this together, ready to share our talents and put our shoulders to the task of making a good life someplace in this world."

Timothy's face grew solemn as he said quietly, "But that is just what I've chosen to do, only here at Oak Abbey. This is the only home I know, but more than that, it's the work I am called to do. We too put our shoulders together, our skills to do whatever good we can here at the Abbey." Brother Timothy's eyes brimmed with tears, but his voice remained steady. "I have found my true brother at last, and I will be forever grateful, but I cannot leave my work, brother."

Overcome, Horace could not speak for a moment. "Well, then," he said at last, "I too must be content with having found you, even if you will not go with us. Perhaps one day you will come to Fleur Gardens, though it is a far journey from here."

Mr. Baxter laid his paw on Horace's shoulder. "It's true, my boy, we have come a good long way from home, but it may be we do not have to take that journey just yet." He stopped to clear his throat. "I didn't sleep much last night for thinking, and I believe there is something we might all think about. Only days from here, though it might as well be years away, those poor cliff dwellers are living without the joy of hope. In our own community I am known as keeper of the stories and traditions of mousedom, stories of joy and courage, traditions that make us who we are. I would like to bring these gifts to those who have not heard them, and perhaps those who once knew but have forgotten. If I may spend time among these cliff mice, perhaps even live out my days there, it will be well with me." He spoke with passion in his voice.

"Now that's a thought," said Max. "I wouldn't mind teaching those fellows how to build decent tunnels, that is if Miss Bea here wouldn't mind teaching a few cooking tricks of hers."

Miss Bea blushed and nodded.

"Oh, Horace," Leta urged, "with your talent for drawing and painting pictures just think of the wonderful things you could teach. Think of the happiness, the freedom you could bring those poor youngsters!"

Horace shook his head in bewilderment. "You mean you would all be willing to go back to the caves? It wouldn't be easy. They're a superstitious lot, and the old one, their chief, may not take to our coming in with changes." Horace twitched his whiskers thoughtfully. "But I can't say it wouldn't be worth our trying. If you're all determined to do this, then I guess you better count me in."

Leta clapped her paws at Horace's announcement.

"Don't count me out," Brother Timothy added. "You say this place is only a few days' journey from here? Why then, Oak Abbey of the gray-friars will be your home away from home. We have medicines and herbs here for the sharing. And if you like, I'm sure Brother Barnabas will give his permission for me to visit now and then." Timothy's kind face lit with pleasure.

Horace wiped his eyes and cleared his throat. "It's settled then; we've accomplished our first quest and begin another."

"And one more thing," Brother Timothy said reaching into his pouch. "This." He held his half of the ivory tree necklace in his hand. Turning to Leta, he said, "Finding my twin brother is enough for me, and now this belongs to you." He placed the necklace around Leta's neck. "I want you to have it to remember me by, and if I'm not mistaken you will soon be a part of this family too."

Horace smiled broadly when Leta ducked her head to hide her warm face.

A hearty voice broke upon the little group as Brother Barnabas rushed up with several large bags in his arms. "You'll need these provisions for your journey, friends," he said, handing the bags to Max and Horace. Resting a paw on Timothy's shoulder, Brother Barnabas smiled. "Go in peace, and may you come again in good health."

Horace swiftly undid his pack and removed a sheet of paper and a piece of charcoal. Quickly and surely he sketched lines and marks. "There," he said holding it up, "a map. If ever you need to find us at the cliffs, this will help show you the way."

Astonishment covered Timothy's face as he took the bit of paper. "You are skilled, brother, in a most wondrous manner," he said. "I shall treasure this."

"Visit us at the cliffs, and I will draw your likeness for you, brother," Horace said. "Not that I should have far to look to remember it," he whispered to himself as the travelers started on their journey. With a final wave of his paw to the two still standing near the abbey door, he turned and began whistling.

One chapter in his life had come to a close with a good ending. What lay ahead was a fresh page waiting for whatever could be drawn upon it.